"In other words, you won't go out with me," he said dryly

Nick gave a throaty laugh. "But I always get what I want, Danielle."

"Wouldn't your mistress have something to say about this?" she taunted.

"No! She doesn't own me—no woman does. But I can be very persistent when I want something," he warned throatily.

"And I can be just as determined myself." Danielle hung up the phone before he could say any more.

She moved to the green-onyx jewelry box in her bedroom and lifted the lid with shaking fingers. The twenty-pound notes inside instantly unfolded, as crisp as the day she'd received them.

Nick Andracas hadn't changed at all. He was still the arrogant bastard who had once paid her two hundred pounds for going to bed with him!

Books by Carole Mortimer

HARLEQUIN PRESENTS

406—BRAND OF POSSESSION
418—THE FLAME OF DESIRE
423—LIVING TOGETHER
430—DEVIL LOVER
437—ICE IN HIS VEINS
443—FIRST LOVE, LAST LOVE
452—SATAN'S MASTER
473—FREEDOM TO LOVE
479—POINT OF NO RETURN
502—ONLY LOVER
510—LOVE'S DUEL
518—BURNING OBSESSION
522—RED ROSE FOR LOVE
531—SHADOWED STRANGER
539—FORGOTTEN LOVER
547—FORBIDDEN SURRENDER
556—ELUSIVE LOVER
564—PASSION FROM THE PAST
571—PERFECT PARTNER
579—GOLDEN FEVER
587—HIDDEN LOVE
594—LOVE'S ONLY DECEPTION
603—CAPTIVE LOVING
611—FANTASY GIRL
619—HEAVEN HERE ON EARTH
627—LIFELONG AFFAIR
636—LOVE UNSPOKEN
645—UNDYING LOVE
651—SUBTLE REVENGE
659—PAGAN ENCHANTMENT
669—TRUST IN SUMMER MADNESS

CAROLE MORTIMER

a past revenge

Harlequin Books

TORONTO • NEW YORK • LONDON
AMSTERDAM • PARIS • SYDNEY • HAMBURG
STOCKHOLM • ATHENS • TOKYO • MILAN

For
John and Matthew

Harlequin Presents first edition April 1985
ISBN 0-373-10780-3

Original hardcover edition published in 1984
by Mills & Boon Limited

CHAPTER ONE

COLDLY grey eyes. *Cruelly* cold grey eyes, and black silk sheets. They were memories that would always be with her when she thought of him. Even more so now!

'Danielle? Danielle!' Lewis repeated impatiently as he still did not get her attention. 'I asked if tomorrow afternoon would be convenient for the initial meeting,' he explained none too patiently still. 'I know you've been trying to finish the Gilbraith portrait for this week.'

'I completed it today,' she revealed reluctantly. 'Although I'm not sure I want to become involved in another one just yet. I had it in mind to take a holiday.'

'Not now, Danielle,' Lewis looked scandalised at the idea, his blond good looks momentarily marred by his worried expression. At thirty Lewis Vaughn looked exactly what he was, a successful businessman. He always dressed impeccably, told Danielle that he didn't like the way art had such a bad name with the public, everyone connected with it, including the agent he was, assumed to be bohemian. Lewis certainly had to be the exception to that rule! 'You did hear who you would be painting?' he said, as if she could not possibly have done and still refuse to do it.

'I heard,' she shattered that illusion instantly, knowing exactly who she was being commissioned to paint, and not liking it one little bit.

'Audra McDonald, Danielle,' he repeated anyway.

'Yes,' she still wasn't impressed.

'Okay, but do you realise who commissioned the portrait?' he encouraged with enthusiasm.

She stiffened slightly, although on the outside she looked as cool as normal. She was a very cool lady, revealed little of her real emotions to any but those closest to her. That circle was very small, didn't even include Lewis, despite the fact that he had been her agent and friend for the last five years, the last two of them very successful for them both, Danielle Smith portraits suddenly becoming the fashion. And yet still Lewis did not see beneath the cool façade, knew only her outward beauty, the silky blonde hair feathered in layers to her shoulders, the emotionless green eyes that hid a multitude of secrets he could not even guess at, her nose short and straight, inclined to freckle in the summer months, her mouth a perfect bow, the full pouting lips usually coloured with a peach lipgloss, a gentle blusher adding colour to her naturally pale cheeks. Her tall slenderness suited the loose tops and fitted denims she habitually wore, although she didn't consider herself to be a bohemian either!

'Yes, I know,' she confirmed flatly, pleased her emotions were under control. She had learnt her lesson well.

'Nicholas Andracas,' Lewis told her unnecessarily. 'He telephoned me personally,' he added in a rather awestruck voice. 'I could hardly believe it when he identified himself as the caller.'

Danielle could understand that, had once known that awed feeling herself. 'And he wants me to paint a portrait of his current mistress?' she arched blonde brows.

'Danielle!'

'Well, what would you have me call her?' she mocked lightly. 'It's public knowledge the two of them have been living together for over a year.'

Lewis looked self-conscious. 'I don't think they're actually cohabiting——'

She gave a splutter of unexpected laughter, and it was all the more beautiful because of it, lighting up her whole face. 'It isn't like you to be so correct, Lewis,' she chided. 'Whether they live together or not they are still lovers.'

He still looked uncomfortable. 'I don't think we should moralise about a prospective client——'

'I'm not about to,' she dismissed, standing up. 'I'm just not sure I want to do this one.' And that wasn't strictly true either, she *knew* she didn't want to do it!

'Why not?' a disappointed Lewis followed her across the room to stand at her side as she stared out of the window. 'God, there's no denying Audra McDonald would make a beautiful subject.'

No, there was no denying that, the actress was very beautiful, but then she would have to be to hold the attention of the rich Greek/American oil tycoon. Nicholas Andracas had a reputation for escorting only beautiful women, and the lovely red-haired actress had lasted longer than most, certainly longer than Danielle, that was for sure. She must have broken all records as far as his women were concerned!

Nick would attract women to him even without his millions, was tall and dark, with a harsh attractiveness that hadn't diminished despite his thirty-eight years. And he had grey eyes, coldly cruel grey eyes.

'I've worked hard this last year, Lewis,' she told him curtly. 'I'd like to take a break now.'

'Can't it wait just another month?'

'It could. . . .'

'Then let it,' he pounced eagerly, looking a little sheepish. 'Actually, I've already told Mr Andracas you're free tomorrow afternoon at two o'clock. I hope that is convenient?'

'It's a little late to ask me that,' she turned on him waspishly, emotion in her eyes now. 'I think you could at least have asked me first.'

'I tried. I've been calling you all afternoon, you were always out.'

Danielle sighed her impatience with that excuse. 'You know I always put the telephone on the machine when I'm working, I can't concentrate with it constantly interrupting me. It wouldn't have hurt you to have told Mr Andracas you couldn't reach me and you would call him back when you had.'

'He isn't the sort of man you keep waiting too long,' Lewis grimaced. 'For anything,' he added with rueful resignation.

She knew all about the forceful arrogance of Nicholas Andracas, she also knew the easy-going Lewis would be no match for the older man. 'I can see that,' she sighed. 'All right, Lewis, I'll see Miss McDonald tomorrow.'

'And Mr Andracas,' he put in hastily. 'He wants to meet you too.'

'Lewis——'

'I know,' he held up his hands defensively. 'It's only necessary for you to meet the subject you're to paint,' he recited parrot-fashion. 'But he's commissioning the portrait. And he's willing to pay a nice fat fee too,' he named an amount that made her eyes widen.

'You know my fees aren't as high as that,' she protested.

'It was the amount he suggested,' Lewis explained.

'It's too much,' she shook her head.

'You haven't tried working with Audra McDonald yet,' he told her ruefully. 'I've heard that isn't always a pleasant experience. You could earn every penny of that money in the circumstances.'

The actress's volatile nature was well known to the gossip columns, and Danielle could well imagine Nicholas Andracas would enjoy the constant challenge of taming such a beautiful shrew. Such a woman would suit his own autocratic nature perfectly.

'Nevertheless,' she told Lewis coolly, revealing none of her inner thoughts. 'He will be charged the usual fee.'

'But Danielle——'

'I hope I've made myself clear, Lewis,' she levelled cool green eyes on him.

He shrugged resignedly, knowing it would do no good to argue with her, especially when he had already won the main battle, that of doing the portrait. 'But you'll see Andracas too?' he had to push this point.

The thought of seeing Nick again after seven years wasn't something she had ever wanted or welcomed, but no one had ever accused her of lacking courage. And it was going to take plenty of that to meet Nicholas Andracas again.

'I'll see him too,' she nodded. 'Now if you

wouldn't mind taking a look at the Gilbraith portrait and then delivering it to his office tomorrow? I understand it's to be a birthday present for his wife. What's the occasion of the Audra McDonald portrait?' she enquired casually.

'Probably the opening of *Broken Dolls* next month,' Lewis followed her through to the studio to study the portrait she had done of Melissa Gilbraith from several casual meetings with the other woman the last few months, all of it done without the other woman's knowledge that she was being painted. Danielle wished the Audra McDonald portrait could be done in the same way! 'I heard Andracas is backing it,' he added dryly.

She had heard the actress was in the process of rehearsing the play for the West End, and it didn't surprise her in the least that the woman's lover was financing it. It was difficult to get money to finance even the most excellent of plays nowadays, Nicholas Andracas wouldn't even notice a dent in his fortune of millions with the hundreds of thousands it would cost to back the play.

'How nice to have a rich and obliging lover,' she said with an uncharacteristic bitchiness.

'Just say the word,' Lewis gave her a leering look.

Danielle gave him a mocking look beneath silky lashes. 'You aren't rich, and I'm certainly not in the market for a lover, obliging or otherwise,' she told him dryly.

'Just my luck,' he grimaced. 'Still, I have to keep trying, one of these days I might catch you in a weak moment. Hey, this is good,' he admired the completed Gilbraith portrait.

For the next few minutes they discussed the merits of the portrait, and as they did so Danielle tried to convince herself that this was just another day in her life, an ordinary day. Only she knew it wasn't, and as soon as Lewis left her the memories came back to haunt her.

She remembered a lot more about Nicholas Andracas than his cold grey eyes and those black silk sheets on his bed, remembered too much for her own peace of mind sometimes. And those memories crowded in on her now.

She hadn't wanted to go to the party, probably wouldn't have done so if her friend Rhea hadn't persuaded her to. The two of them had never got on that well with Carly Daniels when they were all at finishing school together, but the chance to see the other girl's home had been too much of a temptation for them both. Carly was a Greek/American, had driven them all mad in Switzerland with tales of how rich her family was. As the older sister of the oil tycoon they knew Carly's mother was rich in her own right, but she had also married into the Daniels fortune, and Carly never let anyone forget it, even if most of her schoolfriends were her peers. Rhea and Danielle had seen the party invitation at the end of their finishing-school days together as something of a joke, and had decided to go in the same frame of mind.

They had been giggling together like the schoolgirls they had just stopped being as they arrived at the Andracas home, the big L-shaped lounge already full of people.

'I think Carly invited half of London too,' Rhea mocked as they helped themselves to a glass of champagne from one of the numerous circulating waiters.

'Probably. I——' She stared openly as she saw the glowering man standing across the room from them. He was the sort of man anyone would stare at!

'Ellie? Ellie, what is it?' Rhea prompted her impatiently at her continued silence.

She dragged her gaze away with effort from the glowering man, blinking as she looked at her red-haired friend. 'It's——The man over there,' she began again. 'I was just thinking he certainly wasn't at school with us,' she managed to infuse mockery into her voice, although in reality the impact of the man had left her stunned. Her statement was also superfluous. The fact that he was a man meant he couldn't possibly have attended the all-female finishing-school, his age, about thirty to their nineteen also indicating that she had probably never seen him before; her father was quite strict about the men he let her date.

She watched as Rhea turned to look at the man, wondering if she saw the same as she did, the hair so dark it had to be black, brows the same colour jutting out over steely grey eyes, the nose long and straight, the full mouth thinned into a belligerent line as he stared down into a glass which contained something much stronger than the bubbly champagne everyone else was drinking. The black evening suit and white shirt were flimsy camouflage for the leashed power in the body beneath, his six foot plus in height adding to that impression of power, of danger. Danielle, or Ellie as she was known to her friends, had never been so affected by the sight of just one man.

'He looks as if his date stood him up,' she joked to cover the embarrassment she felt at being caught gawking at him like a naive child.

'I doubt any woman has ever stood him up in his life,' Rhea derided softly.

'I doubt it too,' she grimaced, chancing another glance at the man. He had another full glass of what looked like whisky in his hand, drinking it as if it were a particularly nasty medicine he needed to take.

Rhea gave her a curious look. 'You still haven't realised who he is, have you?'

Ellie shrugged. 'Should I know him? Do you?' she asked interestedly; she hadn't known Rhea knew any men like this one.

'Not personally,' her friend shook her head. 'Ellie, *that's* Nick Andracas.'

She looked at Rhea blankly. 'Nick Andracas . . .? Oh!' realisation hit her blushingly, and she turned to look at the man with renewed interest—only to find him looking straight back at her, obviously aware of their interest in him! 'Oh God,' she groaned as she swung her gaze away wildly, looking anywhere but at those coldly mocking grey eyes.

'What is it?' Rhea looked worried by her sudden tension. 'Ellie, what's wrong?'

'What's wrong?' she spoke in a whisper, although she didn't quite know why. 'He looked at me. God, it felt as if he stripped me naked at that one glance!' She gave an involuntary shiver. 'It was the most erotic experience of my life,' she admitted shakily.

'Ellie!' her friend gave a surprised splutter of laughter.

She could understand Rhea's reaction, her statement hadn't been one she would normally have made. But then Nick Andracas wasn't a normal man, and he hadn't induced a normal

reaction within her either. She was still shaking
from that single clash of eyes between them,
although a below-lashes look at him now showed
he had lost interest after that one searing glance,
his attention once again fixed in the bottom of his
whisky glass.

'It's true,' she told Rhea breathlessly. 'He just
looked at me and I—God, it was the weirdest
feeling!'

'It's also dangerous,' her friend warned seriously.
'Stay away from him, Ellie, he——'

'Ah here you both are,' Carly cut in with her
usual intrusive drawl.

'Yes, here we both are,' Rhea replied with dry
sarcasm, not having moved from this spot since
they arrived ten minutes earlier. 'Great party,
Carly,' she added derisively.

'Isn't it,' the raven-haired beauty gushed. 'Even
Uncle Nick managed to put in an appearance,' she
glanced across the room, grimacing slightly.
'Although the mood he's in I'm beginning to wish
he hadn't bothered; he's hardly the life and soul of
the party, is he? You'll have to excuse him, I'm
afraid,' her bright smile flashed over her beautiful
face. 'He had some rather bad news today.'

'Oh?' Rhea asked interestedly.

Carly shrugged dismissively. 'It's nothing important. Enjoy yourselves,' she called gaily before
passing on to more guests, the typical 'social
butterfly'.

'Mm,' Rhea murmured thoughtfully. 'She cut
that conversation off pretty abruptly. I wonder
what's happened that could upset a man like Nick
Andracas?'

'Carly said it was nothing important——'

'Carly can be very close-mouthed when she

wants to be, especially when it comes to protecting her family. None of us knew her brother had been in trouble with the police until we saw it in one of the newspapers,' she reminded Ellie of an incident that had happened earlier in the year.

'I doubt it's anything like that this time,' she shook her head.

'Of course not,' Rhea agreed with impatience. 'He's hardly likely to be involved in drugs. But if ever I saw a man drowning his sorrows it's Nick Andracas.'

Ellie felt nervous about looking at him again, hadn't got over the last time she had, and yet she felt a drawing curiosity about him. 'Even millionaires have their problems,' she teased.

Rhea smiled. 'So they do. Let's forget about Nicholas Andracas and enjoy the party. After all, it's supposed to be for us,' she grinned mischievously.

Forgetting about Nick Andracas wasn't something she found easy to do, although she followed Rhea into the adjoining reception room cheerfully enough, even joining in the dancing when urged to do so. But her thoughts kept drifting back to the gloweringly unhappy man in the other room, wondering if he were still downing whisky as if it were water, even more curious to know what it was that could have affected him that deeply. He didn't appear to be a man that was easily ruffled.

She had an opportunity to see him again when she returned from the bathroom upstairs, saw he was still glowering at people, the glass of whisky still in his hand. As she reached the bottom of the stairs he glanced up, as if sensing her gaze on him, his eyes narrowing, as cold as ice. Ellie repressed another shiver, wondering why this man had such an effect on her, even her legs seeming turned to stone, keeping her rooted to the spot. She watched as Nick Andracas swallowed the last of his whisky with slow deliberation, putting the glass down on a nearby table before walking purposefully towards her. Ellie's eyes widened as he came to stand directly in front of her, so close she could see the black flecks in his eyes, could smell the tang of his aftershave.

'I was thinking of leaving this mad-house, would you like to join me?'

His voice was deep and gravelly, spinning off her nerve endings like an abrasive caress. 'Er——'

'I'd like to leave,' he added when she seemed speechless. 'I'd like you to come with me.'

She was even more taken aback at his lazy insistence. Where did he intend taking her if she did leave with him?

'Well?' he rasped impatiently.

'Mr Andracas——'

His eyes became hooded. 'It would seem you have me at a disadvantage.'

'Ellie,' she supplied breathlessly. 'Ellie Smith.'

'Well, Ellie Smith,' he drawled mockingly. 'Do you want to leave or don't you?'

'I came with a friend——'

'The invitation was for you and you alone,' he bit out. 'And I'm likely to change my mind about that in a minute. I dislike argumentative women.'

Not a patient man, she could see that. But she wanted to go with him, knew she would regret it if she didn't. 'I meant I would just like to tell my friend that I'm leaving,' she told him huskily.

He nodded tersely, as if he didn't really see the need for it. 'I'll wait for you outside.'

All Rhea's pleas for her not to go with him had

been to no avail, and within five minutes she had joined him in the waiting Ferrari, the powerful black car as smoothly dangerous as its owner. He didn't speak as they drove, his expression grim.

He parked the car outside an exclusive block of flats in town, his hand firm beneath her elbow as they entered the building. For the first time Ellie considered the fact that she had left the party with a man she didn't know, that no matter how compellingly attractive she found him that he was still an enigma to her. But suddenly she knew exactly why and where he was taking her!

'Mr Andracas,' she tried to talk to him as they went up in the lift. 'I think I——' her words were cut off as his mouth suddenly crushed down on hers, forcing her body back against the lift wall, grinding his hips against hers to transmit his desire for her.

How long the lift doors stood open into his penthouse apartment she never knew, only that he carried her in there several minutes later, laying her down on the silky sensuousness of black sheets, quickly removing her clothes. Ellie lay watching as he stripped off his own clothes, unable to fight the inevitable, knowing from the moment she looked across that room at him that he was her destiny, that she had fallen in love with him on sight.

He didn't say a word as he made love to her, merely deriving enjoyment from the pleasure he gave her body, his experience undeniable as he took her to each new plateau of ecstasy, making her ready for him before he possessed her with a fierce thrust of his body. If she cried out at that possession she didn't know it, although the pain ripped through her until the world began to spin.

And then passion soared, a sensation such as she had never dreamt existed, and she knew Nick felt the pleasure too as with a groan he crashed through the realms of ecstasy with her.

He moved away from her immediately, the glittering pleasure she had seen alight in his eyes and face as he made love to her now replaced by cynical boredom, his gaze assessing as it swept over her contemptuously. 'I gather you were one of Carly's personal guests?' he finally drawled.

She drowned her puzzlement that he should make the statement so contemptuously, the black silk sheet now pulled up to her chin, although Nick felt no such need to cover his nakedness, stretched out on the bed beside her like a sleek cat. 'How did you guess?' She moistened swollen lips, feeling their tenderness with the tip of her tongue, the rest of her body feeling equally as sore now that desire had faded.

His mouth twisted. 'It wasn't difficult,' he dismissed dryly, standing up, the sleekness of a cat instantly intensified by his grace of movement. He picked up his jacket from the floor where he had thrown it earlier, taking out a cigar case and lighter. 'Do you mind?' he quirked dark brows at her.

She despised the habit of smoking, but she had a feeling his request for permission was only perfunctory, that he didn't really care what her answer was. 'Please do,' she nodded distractedly. 'Does it bother you that I know Carly?'

He looked at the tip of his cigar as smoke curled up to the ceiling. 'Not at all. My little niece may have her parents convinced what a sweet little girl she is, but I happen to know better,' he derided.

So did Ellie, although she wasn't about to go

into the other girl's indiscretions just now. 'What does Carly's behaviour have to do with us?' she frowned.

Cold grey eyes raked over her mercilessly. 'Use your imagination, Ellie Smith,' he mocked. 'Your performance just now may have been a little— mechanical, but I'm sure you have one.'

'I don't understand,' she shook her head, pale at the description he gave to her inexperienced lovemaking.

'A complete stranger comes up to you at a party and asks you to leave with him, you agree, and you now ask how I know you know Carly,' he scorned harshly, pulling on the black silk robe that lay over a chair. 'What are you, a consolation gift from my dear little niece?' he made the words an insult.

Ellie was so pale now her eyes looked as dark as emeralds, her long hair tangled down her back. 'Consolation gift?' she repeated dazedly.

His expression was grim. 'It's just the sort of thing that little madam would do,' he rasped. 'And I'm glad she chose someone like you.' He looked at her once again. 'Anyone remotely resembling my wife would have turned me off completely.' He stubbed his cigar out in the ashtray with vicious movements.

'Your—your wife?' She felt as if someone had just dealt her a painful body blow.

'You can cut the cute little act now, Ellie,' he derided. 'I realise Carly asked you to send me those charming little messages across the room with your eyes to help me forget the fact that my wife served me with divorce papers today. And it has helped,' he nodded, his eyes narrowed. 'Now get your beautiful little body out of my bed,' he bent down to slap her bottom hard. 'I don't want you any more tonight, pleasant as the experience may have been.'

Ellie had never felt so mortified in her entire life. She had had no idea until now that he had misunderstood her coy glances at him earlier, but she now knew the reason for the desperate drive behind his possession, realised that the 'bad news' he had received today had been his wife's intention of divorcing him.

She could only stare at him now, not knowing how to defend herself. It was obvious he thought her as promiscuous as she knew Carly to be, that he thought the two of them had planned together that she should share his bed as a way of helping him forget his impending divorce. It was also obvious that he had mistaken her virginity and inexperience as a mechanical response to his lovemaking, so how was she now supposed to tell him she had fallen in love with him on sight, that he had taken her virginity! She couldn't, not when he saw her only as a mild diversion in his bed.

'I'm going to take a shower now,' he told her. 'You can use the other bathroom if you want to, but I want you to have left by the time I get back.' He picked up his jacket for a second time, taking out a leather wallet, pulling several notes from inside it, putting them on the dressing-table. 'Take a cab home,' he ordered. 'I don't feel like going out again tonight, and I don't want you walking alone at this time of night.'

'Please——'

'Not enough?' he raised dark brows mockingly, misunderstanding the reason for her protest. 'Maybe not,' he acknowledged with a humourless smile. 'But you aren't very experienced at this sort of thing yet. Complacence may have been what I wanted tonight, but I can assure you most men will want more than that. Maybe you could give me a call when you've learnt to show a little more fire and enthusiasm,' he dismissed derisively, pausing at the door. 'And don't try and rip me off once I've gone to shower,' he warned in a pleasantly threatening voice. 'I'll have you arrested so fast you won't know what's hit you.' He closed and locked the bathroom door behind him, the shower running seconds later.

Ellie had listened to him with increasing wide-eyed incredulity, the reality of what he thought her to be becoming apparent by the second. He certainly didn't believe her to be a *friend* of Carly's! She moved slowly from the bed to pick up the money he had thrown down so casually, counting it as if in a dream. Two hundred pounds!

Danielle came back to shuddering reality, the humiliation she had suffered at Nicholas Andracas's hands that night something she had never forgotten. It had been the first time in her nineteen years that someone had treated her with such contempt, and although he may have forgotten her existence in the last seven years— may have forgotten her the moment he entered that bathroom for all she knew!—she had never forgotten him, not even for a day.

The news of Nick's divorce had hit the newspapers a couple of days after she met him, his wife accusing him of adultery several times over. After her own experience with him she could quite well believe that Beverley Andracas probably deserved the millions of dollars she received in settlement from him. Any woman who could stay married to such a man for four years deserved everything she could get out of him.

But her main worry now was whether or not he would recognise Danielle Smith, successful portrait painter, as Ellie Smith, the girl he had once paid for going to bed with him? God, that must have been a novel experience for him, he had probably never paid a woman for sex in his life before! He would never need to.

But she was still worrying about whether he would recognise her as she waited for him and Audra McDonald to arrive at her apartment the next afternoon. If he didn't remember her she could carry out this meeting with some degree of dignity, but if he should remember her . . .! The consequences of that didn't bear thinking about, and she tried not to.

When the doorbell rang promptly at two o'clock she took her time about answering it, checking her appearance in the mirror one last time. The denims and loose green top weren't an act of defiance on her part, more a need to be wearing something so completely different than the sophisticated black evening gown she had been wearing the last time she met Nick Andraças. Her outward appearance had changed the last seven years, her hair was styled shorter now, her once slightly rounded face smoothed out to high cheekbones and angled features, her whole bearing one of maturity now rather than a raw adolescence.

She deliberately trained her attention on Audra McDonald as she opened the door, ignoring the man who stood arrogantly at her side, although she was instantly aware of him, sensing that same charged electricity she had known in him seven years ago. Audra McDonald was as beautiful as her photographs proclaimed her to be, although the sharp brown eyes were narrowed assessingly on Danielle, as if gauging her attractiveness, the brief contempt registered there dismissing her as unimportant. That suited Danielle perfectly, she wanted as little tension and unpleasantness from this commission as possible.

Although she wasn't sure she could count on that to continue as she took the other couple through to the lounge, turning to find the brown eyes were no longer scornfully dismissing, snapping with anger now as Audra McDonald saw and recognised her lover's open interest in Danielle. Danielle was forced to recognise it too as she also met the warmth in narrowed grey eyes.

Nick had changed little in the last seven years, the black hair showing flecks of grey, the cynicism in his expression deepened, but otherwise he was the same devastatingly attractive man she had once fallen instantly in love with. She felt a similar leap of her senses to the one she had felt that night, although she remained outwardly cool and uninterested, maturity showing her how best to handle this meeting.

'Do you have any idea what sort of portrait you would like?' she addressed her question to Audra McDonald, although she wasn't altogether surprised when Nick Andracas answered.

'We know exactly what sort of portrait we want, Miss Smith,' he told her smoothly. 'It's a requirement of the play Miss McDonald is in, and will be presented to her at the end of the play's run.'

'Oh,' she nodded understanding, giving no indication that his gravelly sensuous voice meant anything to her, her interest wholly professional as she listened to him explain the details of the portrait needed.

'You have precisely one month to complete the portrait to our requirements, Miss Smith,' he finally concluded. 'We need it for the opening night.'

'Of course,' she acknowledged stiltedly. 'I'll do my best.'

'And I'm sure that will be good enough,' he returned huskily, his eyes darkly caressing.

She refused to meet that gaze, deliberately turning to the actress who had sat quietly at his side on the sofa as he talked. 'When would you like to begin your sittings, Miss McDonald?'

Anger still burned deep in the brown eyes. 'Is that really necessary?' she drawled in a bored voice. 'Wouldn't a photograph do?'

Danielle shook her head, all the time aware that narrowed grey eyes never left her face. But they contained no grain of recognition of the past, she was sure of that, saw her only as the beautiful woman she was now. 'I'm afraid I can't work that way,' she explained politely. 'Although I could recommend someone else who——'

'No,' Nick Andracas cut in abruptly. 'I want you to do the portrait.'

'Really, Nick,' Audra McDonald turned to him impatiently, her beautiful mouth pouting provocatively. 'Do I have to sit around here for hours on end, bored out of my mind?'

'Yes,' his answer was uncompromising.

Her hand came to rest on his thigh. 'I'd much rather spend the time with you.'

He looked at her without emotion. 'You'll come here as often as Miss Smith requires you to.'

'But, Nick——'

'Audra!' He didn't raise his voice, he didn't need to, his tone enough to silence his mistress.

Danielle witnessed the exchange with a certain amount of embarrassment. That the fiery Audra McDonald was about as 'tamed' as she could be when with this man was obvious, her expression now rebellious, although she raised no more objections. Danielle did not like the other woman in the least, but she could feel sorry for her. 'I doubt I'll need to trouble you for more than one or two sittings,' again she ignored Nick Andracas, talking to the actress. 'And probably only for an hour or so at a time, perhaps on a Saturday morning if that's convenient?'

Brown eyes shot Nick Andracas a resentful glare, although he seemed immune to it. 'I suppose Saturday is all right,' she agreed ungraciously. 'Although it will have to be in the afternoon,' she gave her lover a smouldering look from beneath long lashes. 'I don't like to get out of bed early.'

'What time is most convenient for you, Miss Smith?' Nick Andracas ignored the actress's effort to flirt with him, removing her hand pointedly from his thigh, his mouth a thin straight line of disapproval at the intimacy.

Danielle was beginning to get the feeling she had been brought in on the middle of a lovers' tiff. Or perhaps this was the way Nick always treated his mistress? He had been cruel and unfeeling in the past, perhaps those emotions had just intensified with the passing of the years. 'The afternoon will be fine,' she said coolly. 'About two o'clock?'

He nodded. 'I believe Mr Vaughn has told you the details of your fee?' he raised dark brows in challenge, as if he already knew of her refusal to accept the amount he had offered.

'It's too much,' she met his challenge. 'You will get the bill for the usual amount once the portrait is completed. If my work is satisfactory.'

The grey eyes rekindled with interest. 'I'm sure it will be.'

'Only time will tell.' She had a feeling Audra McDonald wasn't going to be an easy subject to paint. Besides the fact that she didn't actually like the other woman, there was the problem of her brittle hardness to contend with, a quality they didn't want in the portrait, she felt sure. 'I——' she broke off as the telephone began to ring, surmising it to be Lewis wanting to know how the meeting had gone. He was a little premature. 'Excuse me,' she gave a bright meaningless smile in the other couple's direction before picking up the receiver.

'Ellie?'

She instantly recognised her father's voice, some of the tension leaving her. 'How are you?' she asked warmly, listening as he went on to tell her briefly about the holiday he and her mother had just taken. 'Dinner tonight?' she repeated his suggestion. 'That would be lovely.' She rang off a few minutes later, turning to find narrowed grey eyes levelled on her, displeasure etched into the harsh features. 'Sorry about that,' she felt compelled to make the apology. 'Now where were we?'

'I believe we had just about concluded the meeting,' Nick Andracas rasped harshly, standing up, the three-piece suit in charcoal grey fitting his lithe masculinity to perfection. 'Miss McDonald will be here at two o'clock on Saturday.'

The other couple left so abruptly Danielle was left with a sense of anti-climax, although she had to admit to a certain amount of relief too. The meeting had been as much of a strain as she had thought it would be, although at least she had been spared the humiliation of recognition. Nick had seen her only as Danielle Smith, although there could be no doubt that he found her attractive in that capacity. He was a dangerous man for any woman to find attractive, had been lethal for her all those years ago.

When the telephone rang half an hour later she felt sure that this time it had to be Lewis. It was not.

'Danielle, will you have dinner with me this evening?'

There was no need for him to identify himself, she recognised his voice immediately. 'I'm sorry, Mr Andracas, I already have an appointment this evening,' she refused frostily, a telephone call from him so soon after he had left the last thing she had been expecting.

'So I heard,' he bit out. 'I want you to break it.'

Now she knew the reason for his abruptness before he left. She had thought he had been annoyed that she had taken the telephone call while he was here, instead he had been eager to drop off his mistress so that *he* could ask her for a date! The cold-blooded arrogance of the man. 'I'm afraid that's out of the question.' She thought back on the conversation he had overheard, realising that not once had she identified her caller as her father. 'I really couldn't let my friend down at such short notice,' she added with throaty insinuation.

For a moment there was angry silence on the other end of the telephone. 'Tomorrow?' he finally rasped.

'I'm afraid not.'

'You're seeing the same man again then?'

'Possibly,' she evaded lying.

'In other words you don't wish to go out with me?' he said dryly.

'That's right,' she acknowledged coldly.

He gave a throaty laugh at her honesty. 'But I always get what *I* want, Danielle. And I wanted you the moment I set eyes on you.'

'Wouldn't Miss McDonald have something to say about this?' she taunted with sarcasm.

'No,' he answered abruptly. 'She wouldn't. She doesn't own me, no woman does.'

'I'm really very sorry, Mr Andracas,' she snapped. 'But I really have no desire to go out with you, either now or in the forseeable future.'

'I can be very persistent when I want something,' he warned throatily.

'And I can be just as determined myself. Goodbye, Mr Andracas,' she rang off before he could say any more, sitting down abruptly. He hadn't changed at all, was still the arrogant bastard who had once paid her to go to bed with him.

She moved dazedly into her bedroom, going straight to the green onyx jewellery box that stood on her dressing-table, lifting the lid with shaking fingers. The twenty pound notes inside instantly unfolded, as crisply new as the day she had received them. Danielle had no need to count them, she already knew exactly how much money there was there.

After Nick had gone into the shower that night she had dressed in a daze before leaving, not realising until she reached home and the sanctuary of her bedroom that she had stuffed the ten twenty pound notes which Nick had so contemptuously tossed at her in her handbag. At first she had wanted to take it straight back, but the thought of facing his mocking derision for a second time that night hadn't appealed to her at all in her still shocked state. She decided to post it back to him. By morning she had changed her mind about that, deciding to keep the money as a reminder of the man who had paid her two hundred pounds for her virginity. And she had never forgotten him, hated him now as she had hated him then.

CHAPTER TWO

THE telephone calls persisted over the next three days, every couple of hours or so, and each time Nick asked her to go out with him. When she switched her answering machine on permanently so as to avoid talking to him the flowers started to arrive, dozens and dozens of them. She sent them straight to a local hospital, telling the florist to tell Mr Andracas what she had done with them. No more flowers arrived. She was waiting for his next move now. She was not expecting it to be quite the one he did make, although she had a feeling he could be unpredictable. He was standing on the doorstep with Audra McDonald when she opened the door Saturday afternoon!

'Don't worry, Miss Smith,' he drawled at her suddenly wary look. 'I'm not staying. I only came to discuss a few details with you that we overlooked the other day.'

She could imagine what 'details' they were, although with Audra McDonald listening to their every word she could hardly refuse to let him in. Much as she would like to! Mocking grey eyes seemed to know exactly how she felt, her voice waspish as she invited the couple inside.

'If you would just like to go somewhere and change, Audra,' Nick suggested smoothly. 'I just want to talk to Miss Smith for a few minutes.'

'I can change once you've gone,' she actress dismissed.

'It would save time if you do it now,' he arched dark brows in challenge.

With a dark flash of resentment she turned to Danielle with furious eyes. 'Do you have somewhere I might change?'

She frowned at the request. 'What you're wearing is perfectly suitable——'

'I have to be wearing a gown from the play,' the other woman snapped her impatience.

'Oh.' She hadn't realised that. 'Well, there's my studio. Or my bedroom,' she added with a certain amount of reluctance.

Audra chose the bedroom, as Danielle had known she would, leaving her alone in there while she came back to face Nick Andracas.

'You wanted to talk to me?' she looked up at him with cool enquiry as he seemed in no hurry to speak, merely staring at her with open interest.

His mouth twisted, his hands thrust into the pockets of his black fitted trousers, his shirt the same steel grey as his eyes. 'I've been trying to talk to you all week, you know that.'

'I thought this conversation was going to be business, Mr Andracas,' she turned away.

'It is,' he bit out. 'Vaughn tells me you've remained adamant about your fee?'

She stiffened. 'That's right.'

He eyed her curiously. 'I've never known anyone turn down money before.'

'Really?' she bit out between taut lips, knowing her own behaviour in the past had added to his disillusionment.

'Really,' he nodded.

'Then this must be a pleasant change for you, mustn't it,' her voice was brittle.

'It might be if I understood the reason for it.'

Her eyes darkened to the colour of emeralds. 'I know my worth, Mr Andracas, and I won't take a penny more than that.'

'Not even if it's offered to you?' he seemed puzzled by her vehemence.

'No,' she snapped. 'Money isn't everything, Mr Andracas, I'm surprised you haven't learnt that yet.'

'Yet?' his eyes narrowed with suspicion.

She shrugged, realising her slip in her anger. 'You've been wealthy all your life, it doesn't seem to have brought you much happiness,' she dismissed.

'How do you know that?' he rasped.

'I read the newspapers, Mr Andracas,' she told him coolly. 'You're often mentioned.'

'And what have you learnt about me from them?' he queried softly, too softly.

'That you've had one broken marriage and don't seem to ever want to contemplate another one.'

'You consider marriage the only happiness in life?' he arched dark brows. 'In that case, why haven't you married?' he said with barely concealed sarcasm, evidence of how her remarks had caught him on the raw, the subject of his previous marriage obviously not something he liked to talk about.

She turned away. 'The man I loved didn't ask me,' she replied woodenly.

'Your dining companion of the other evening?' he rasped.

'No,' she bit out, the evening spent with her parents at their home as pleasant as usual.

'Then I have a ghost from your past to contend with as well as your present lover,' he realised dryly.

'No ghost, Mr Andracas,' she assured him waspishly. 'I got over the stupidity of that love a long time ago, a very long time ago,' she repeated forcefully. 'And there's no lover now either, only friends.'

He frowned darkly. 'Then why do you persistently refuse my invitations?'

'You already have one mistress, Mr Andracas,' she reminded with contempt. 'Can't you be satisfied with her? She certainly seems satisfied with you,' she mocked.

His hands clenched at his sides. 'I want *you*, damn it,' he rasped fiercely.

'I'm sorry.'

'Are you?' he swung her round as she would have turned away from him, his gaze raking mercilessly over her emotionless face. 'I don't think you're sorry at all.'

'Probably not,' she shrugged.

His face twisted with fury, giving him an almost satanic look. 'What do you want from me?'

She met his gaze coldly. 'I'm not for sale, if that's what you mean.'

'Everyone has their price!'

'Do you?'

He looked taken aback for a moment, then he dropped her arm to turn away. 'No,' he answered abruptly. 'But women are different,' he added insultingly.

'Are they?' she still remained calm, although inside she was burning with indignation. 'Then I would say you've been associating with the wrong type of woman—or the right sort, depending which way you look at it.'

'I could ruin you and your career with a few choice words in the right direction!'

Danielle shrugged, immune to any threats he might make. 'What you're talking about is blackmail, Mr Andracas,' she pointed out softly. 'And that isn't a price. You were talking about greed just now, not survival.'

'Are you always this damned logical?' he rasped impatiently.

'I'm just myself, Mr Andracas. And thankfully women now have a choice in this world, we don't have to be treated like possessions or second-class citizens any more.'

'In other words, you're an independent lady and intend to stay that way,' he drawled.

'As I said,' she gave a cool inclination of her head. 'I'm just me.'

He sighed his chagrin. 'And what am I supposed to do about the fact that I desire you?'

'Take a cold shower?' she taunted.

'Why you little——'

'Please,' she mocked with confidence, knowing he was more amused than angry. 'Let's not resort to insults.'

'Let's not talk at all,' he rasped, coming threateningly towards her.

Danielle remembered him as having more control than this, had never dreamt that her taunts would lead to this, shrinking away from him as he took her into his arms.

'Nick darling, I——' Audra McDonald came to an astounded halt in the doorway, her gaze moving over them both with glittering accusation.

Danielle released herself with a relief the other woman couldn't realise, although by the angry narrowing of Nick's eyes he knew exactly how she felt—and he didn't like it. She didn't give a damn what he liked, and she never would!

'What a beautiful gown,' she admired the red dress the other woman wore, the colour of a shade that enhanced rather than clashed with her flaming red hair. It would make a very dramatic effect on canvas.

The other woman ignored the compliment, her gaze fixed on her lover. 'I can't quite reach the top hook, Nick,' she told him curtly. 'Could you do it for me?'

He moved across the room with forceful strides, dealing with the hook in a matter of seconds. 'I'll be back to pick you up in an hour's time,' he told the actress, looking over at Danielle, the mask of control firmly back in place. 'Will that be convenient for you, Miss Smith?'

'An hour will be fine,' she nodded, as coolly indifferent now as he was.

'See you later, darling,' Audra put her arms about his neck to kiss him lingeringly on the lips.

He made no effort to end the kiss, his arms about the actress's waist, the kiss long and leisurely. Danielle ignored the triumphant challenge in his eyes as he at last broke the embrace, looking at him coldly, although the kiss seemed to have placated Audra McDonald, lazy satisfaction in her smile now.

Not that the emotion seemed to last once they were alone in the studio, the brown eyes flashing with dislike as Danielle posed the other woman in the chair.

'It won't work, Miss Smith,' Audra finally snapped.

She had been expecting the attack ever since Nick Andracas left, concentrating on the sketch she was doing, not at all disturbed by the other woman's anger. 'What won't?' she asked uninterestedly.

'Nick and I have been together a long time,' Audra more or less purred. 'I know how to keep him satisfied.'

'Good.'

'He has his little flirtations from time to time, of course,' the other woman laughed them off as of no importance. 'But he always comes back to me.'

'That must make you very happy,' Danielle answered in a preoccupied voice.

'It does,' Audra snapped defensively.

She shrugged. 'Then that's all right, isn't it?'

'Don't look so smug, Miss Smith,' Audra rasped. 'He may find you attractive now, but it won't last.'

'I hope not,' she said quietly, the sketch not going quite as well as she wanted it to. 'Could you please sit perfectly still while I do this?' The other woman was moving about in her agitation. 'It's difficult for me to sketch you if you don't.'

'That can wait for a few minutes,' Audra dismissed impatiently. 'Are you trying to tell me you don't find Nick attractive?' she sounded sceptical.

Danielle sighed, nodding. 'That's exactly what I'm telling you, Miss McDonald.'

'I don't believe you!'

'Oh I should,' she mocked. 'Because it's the truth. Not every woman finds him as attractive as you do,' she added dryly.

'I've never met one yet who didn't!'

'You just did,' Danielle snapped.

'And that little scene I witnessed between you a few minutes ago?' Audra reminded waspishly.

'I agree with you that it was a scene,' she sighed. 'But it wasn't between us, as you suggest it was, it was all Mr Andracas' idea.'

Audra frowned. 'You really don't like him?' she made it sound as if that were impossible.

'Not in the least,' she replied flatly.

'Don't you realise the challenge of that will only make him more interested than ever?'

'What are you suggesting I do?' she mocked. 'Pretend an interest in him I don't feel just to get him to leave me alone?'

The other woman flushed. 'Of course not,' she bit out. 'That would be stupid.'

'Yes, it would.' And it was something she could never do.

The brown eyes narrowed. 'I'm very much afraid that I don't like you, Miss Smith,' Audra said slowly.

Danielle was very much afraid she didn't like the other woman either. Audra seemed to be an intelligent woman, seemed to regard Nick Andracas as an asset in her life rather than the man she was actually in love with. Maybe the two of them deserved each other!

'Do you have to?' she raised mocking brows at the other woman. 'I mean, is it necessary?'

'No, thank God,' Audra's mouth twisted disgustedly. 'Let's get on with this damned portrait.'

This 'damned portrait' was probably going to be the hardest piece of work Danielle had ever done. It was not just the hardness of the other woman's features that was making it difficult, it was also the actress's attitude. Audra was not at all enthusiastic about being painted in the first place, was very restless in the chair, and Nick Andracas had further complicated matters by making the other woman resent her before they had even begun.

It was a difficult hour, and Danielle felt drained

at the end of it, her main feeling one of relief when
the doorbell rang shortly after three. Although she
wasn't looking forward to seeing Nick again,
hadn't realised he would continue to be quite so
involved, knowing that he didn't need to be after
that initial meeting, that he had chosen to do so.

She went to answer the door while Audra used
her bedroom once again to get changed. That was
something else she didn't like about this commission. With the studio being in her home she
naturally had a certain amount of invasion of her
privacy, but her bedroom had always remained
apart from that before, none of her other clients
needing to change before she painted them.
Although she could understand the other woman's
reluctance to arrive in the gown; it was for evening
wear, not for driving about London on a sunny
Saturday afternoon. But even so, Danielle couldn't
say she exactly liked the other woman using what
was, after all, her own personal room.

Nick looked much the same as he had an hour
ago when she opened the door to him, tall and
arrogant, striding confidently into her home. 'You
look tired,' he turned to say bluntly.

She knew exactly how she looked—and felt. Her
hair was tousled into disorder, her face slightly
pale from the intensity of the work she had been
doing the last hour, the peach lipgloss all but gone
from her mouth where she had been chewing her
lips in concentration. 'And I had been led to
believe you were a very charming man,' she
mocked.

His eyes narrowed. 'By whom?'

'Guess,' her mouth twisted.

'Audra,' he derided. 'Did she tell you that before
or after she warned you off me?'

Her mouth tightened at his astuteness. 'During, I think,' she taunted.

'I see,' he drawled. 'And did you tell her the warning was unnecessary?'

'Of course,' she replied with sarcasm. 'I made very sure she knows I have no interest in you whatsoever,' she added insultingly, hating his arrogance all over again, his self-satisfaction about how the other woman would react to seeing them together earlier.

'Then you may have done me a favour, Miss Smith,' he taunted.

'Oh?' she eyed him cautiously, knowing she wouldn't offer him help if he were bleeding to death, that she hated him enough to stand and watch.

'Audra is inclined to be a little bit more— attentive, when she believes, erroneously or not, that she has competition,' he eyed her mockingly.

Danielle flushed as his meaning became clear. 'Then I mustn't keep either of you any longer than necessary,' she dismissed coldly. 'I'll go and see if Miss McDonald is ready to leave yet.'

'Danielle!' His fingers bit into her arm as he dragged her round to face him.

'Take your hands off me, Mr Andracas,' she instructed in an icy voice, not at all surprised when he, with a chagrined frown, released her. She looked at him with cool disdain. 'Your affair with Miss McDonald is your business,' she told him emotionlessly. 'As is the way you treat her,' she added contemptuously. 'But I will not be used by you as a means of making her jealous, and so more *attentive*. Do I make myself clear?'

'As crystal,' he drawled unconcernedly.

'Good,' she nodded. 'Because I would also like

to add that you have hired my services as a portrait painter, nothing else. And if you can't, or won't, accept that, then I suggest you get yourself someone else for the job.'

He gave an exaggerated sigh of relief that her tirade was over. 'You can really let fly when you want to, can't you,' he mused, his arms folded in front of his powerful chest.

'When I *have* to,' she corrected pointedly, hating his condescending attitude to her anger.

He quirked dark brows over mocking eyes. 'And with me you have to?'

'With you I'm going to,' she told him firmly. 'I want to make it clear once and for all that I'm not interested in being one of your little diversions. I value myself a lot higher than some rich, bored man's mistress for a few weeks.'

'My wealth I can't deny,' he shrugged. 'But what makes you think I'm bored?'

'What makes you think you're not?' she instantly returned.

For the first time since she had ever met him he gave a genuinely amused smile. 'You're very astute, Danielle,' he drawled dryly. 'I am bored. I have competent men to run my businesses for me, that leaves me to the enjoyment of life.'

'Then it's a pity you don't actually enjoy it,' she told him waspishly. 'And leave me alone.'

'Danielle——'

'I'm ready to leave now, Nick,' Audra spoke softly from behind them. 'If you are,' she added brittly, seeming aware of the tension between them.

'Could you come back next Saturday at the same time?' Danielle requested briskly.

The other woman gave her a look of glittering dislike. 'I'll look forward to it.'

It was a warning, Danielle knew that, but she shrugged it off. 'I believe all our business together is now concluded, Mr Andracas,' she met his steely gaze steadily. 'All that remains is for me to send you the bill when I've completed my work.'

The hardness in his eyes told her that he knew exactly what she was saying—and that he didn't like it one little bit. 'Very well, Miss Smith,' he acquiesed to her unspoken desire not to see him again. 'Goodbye!' he rasped angrily.

She felt drained once she was alone, hadn't missed the triumphant gleam in Audra McDonald's eyes when Nick showed his fury with her. Danielle had a feeling the other woman hadn't believed her non-interest in Nick earlier. Well there could be no doubt that she believed her now!

And so, hopefully, did Nick Andracas. She knew she would only be able to take so much from him, and then she would break under the strain. And if that happened she had no idea what she might do. So far she had managed to keep her hate to a cold dislike, if the coldness ever left her she was afraid she wouldn't be able to control the hate.

'Mmm, I needed that,' Danielle drank some of her wine, at once feeling a soothing glow.

'Rough day?' Lewis sympathised, the two of them having a quiet dinner together at a popular club and restaurant.

'Rough week,' she grimaced, having accepted Lewis's invitation eagerly this morning when he telephoned, glad to get out for a few hours.

'It's only Tuesday,' he teased.

'Is it?' she sighed. 'It seems like this week has lasted for ever.' Not hearing from Nick Andracas was worse than his constant telephone calls. It was like waiting for the axe to fall.

'Some weeks are like that,' he shrugged. 'How is the beautiful Audra's portrait coming along?'

'Slowly,' she admitted heavily. 'She isn't as easy a subject as you would think.'

'I warned you she can be difficult. Changed your mind about the fee?' he mocked.

She shook her head, having had this conversation with him once before. 'It isn't hard that way,' she assured him. 'Admittedly she isn't the easiest of people to get along with, but that isn't what makes this difficult. If I paint her as I see her then she isn't going to like it.'

'Flatter her,' Lewis advised with his usual eye for business first, art later.

'Then she may be unrecognisable,' Danielle pulled a face.

He laughed softly at her dilemma. 'I'm sure you'll find a compromise that will satisfy everyone.'

She liked his confidence in her capabilities, but she wasn't altogether sure it was true this time; the portrait was proving to be as difficult to do as she had predicted to herself that it would.

She ran a hand across her nape as she felt a prickly sensation, unconsciously massaging the spot. But the sensation continued, so much so that she was beginning to feel very uncomfortable, wondering if she had been bitten by something.

'Talk of the devil,' Lewis muttered.

'Hm?'

He nodded across the room from them. 'Andracas and Miss McDonald,' he murmured.

She turned sharply to find Nick and Audra seated a short distance away from them, the reason for the prickly sensation at her nape obvious now as she saw the narrowed grey eyes levelled on her. She looked away abruptly, realising she was still being stared at, still able to feel his gaze on her. The first time she had been out for weeks, the first time she had ever been out with Lewis on a social level, and this had to happen! She was beginning to get the feeling fate had suddenly turned against her.

'What bad luck,' Lewis obviously felt the same way. 'I suppose we'll have to ask them to join us.'

'Why?' she asked sharply.

He looked puzzled by the question, shrugging lightly. 'It's only polite——'

'I don't see why,' she snapped. 'They haven't asked *us* to join them!'

'Danielle——'

'Well, have they?' she prompted.

'They only came in a few minutes ago,' he explained softly.

She sighed. 'I'd rather not eat with them, if you don't mind.'

'But I can't just pretend they aren't there.' He obviously did mind!

'Lewis,' her voice was throatily soft. 'I thought you wanted to be alone with me tonight?'

He flushed. 'I do——'

'Then let's just act as if we haven't seen them, hm?' she touched his hand across the table.

'But I can see them as clearly as——'

'No, you can't, Lewis,' she persuaded, giving him a dazzling smile.

'I—I can't?' he was mesmerised by the warmth of her smile.

'No——'

'Good evening, Danielle, Vaughn,' a familiar

gravelly sounding voice greeted them. 'Audra and I wondered if you would care to join us for dinner?'

Danielle snatched her hand away from Lewis's as if he had burnt her, looking up reluctantly at the man who now stood beside their table, her stomach giving a sickening lurch at how similar he looked in the black evening suit and snowy white shirt to the man she had first seen seven years ago. It was almost unnatural, no time seeming to have passed at all.

His eyes narrowed at how pale she had suddenly become. 'Did I startle you?' he asked in a puzzled voice, as if he wasn't used to having this effect on women.

'No more than usual,' she answered abruptly, 'and as you can see, Lewis and I have already started our meal,' she refused his invitation before Lewis could accept, knowing she had to stay away from him tonight, that she was feeling too vulnerable at the moment to deal with him with her usual coolness.

'Then perhaps you wouldn't mind if the two of us joined you,' he returned smoothly.

'I——'

'Please do,' Lewis cut in firmly as she would have refused once again. 'What's the matter with you?' he demanded in a fierce whisper as Nick Andracas crossed the room to bring Audra McDonald over to their table.

'It must be obvious,' she glared at him. 'I didn't want them to join us!'

'Oh it was obvious, all right,' he snapped impatiently. 'To Andracas too!'

Her mouth twisted. 'I'm sure he's enjoying the fact that he got his way in spite of that!'

'Danielle, he's a client——'

'I'm well aware of what he is, Lewis,' she told him tautly. 'And his being a client is the least important of them.'

He looked puzzled by her unusual behaviour, although he couldn't question her further as the other couple joined them, standing up politely until they were seated.

From what Danielle could gather from Audra's stilted manner as they ate dinner the other woman was no more eager for the foursome than she was. Only Nick seemed perfectly at ease with the arrangement, Lewis talking incessantly to try and cover the obvious silence of the two women.

Although both women declined Nick's suggestion that they all go upstairs and dance they somehow found themselves in the smoky atmosphere of the nightclub, a table for four miraculously secured for them, despite the fact that the place was crowded.

'Would you care to dance, Danielle?'

Her heart sank at the request she had known was coming, the last thing she wanted was to be in Nick's arms again, for any reason. 'I think it's a little soon after I've eaten,' she refused.

'Perhaps later,' he nodded, the mockery in his eyes telling her that he knew it was just an excuse, that he knew she didn't want to dance with him, the fact that she had hardly eaten anything at all telling him she was merely prevaricating.

'Perhaps,' she agreed, both of them knowing that it would take a miracle for her to dance with him, or something equally as effective—and Nick Andracas was certainly that. After she had refused to dance with him the third time she could see Lewis was becoming really uncomfortable with the situation, asking Audra to dance as a diversion. With a certain amount of reluctance for leaving the two of them alone together Audra followed Lewis out on to the dance floor.

Nick moved his chair closer to Danielle's, his leg partially touching hers under the table. 'Alone at last,' he mocked her desire to have nothing to do with him.

She looked at him uninterestedly. 'It would seem so,' she acknowledged without enthusiasm.

'You aren't going to excuse yourself to the powder-room, or something equally boring?'

She flushed at his mockery. 'No,' she answered tautly.

'But you still don't want to dance?'

'No,' she said again.

'You're consistent, I'll say that for you. Or is it just that you prefer not to dance with anyone but Vaughn?' he leant back in his chair, perfectly relaxed, smoke swirling up to the ceiling from the cigar he held in his right hand.

'Lewis?' her brows rose questioningly. 'But I haven't danced with him either.'

'You're having dinner with him.'

'Yes.'

'Is he your lover?'

She was taken aback at the question, although she didn't show it, her expression as composed as usual. 'What if he is?' she asked coldly.

'I——'

'Goodness, it's hot out there,' Audra complained as she and Lewis returned to the table before the music had ended.

Nick stood up abruptly, pulling Danielle with him out on to the dance floor, moulding her firmly to his body as they barely moved in time to the music.

'You didn't have to do that,' she told him between stiff lips, her hands on his chest trying to keep them apart—and failing miserably.

'I hadn't finished talking to you,' he told her with his usual arrogance. 'Is Vaughn your lover?'

'I don't have to answer that,' she averted her face from his.

'Yes, you do,' he ground out. 'You lied to me, and no woman does that!'

Suddenly she was free of him, but they were no longer in the crowded club, Nick having somehow manoeuvred it so that they were outside on the darkened roof garden, strategically placed flood-lights on the lush green plants the only illumination out there.

'I want to go back inside——'

'No!' his eyes glittered dangerously. 'You told me you didn't have a lover——'

'I don't!'

'I don't believe you! Women are liars at birth,' he bit out harshly, his hands firm on her arms as he pulled her closer to him.

'Why would I need to lie?' she demanded disgustedly. 'To do that I would have to be interested in you enough to want to lie, and I'm not.'

'Aren't you?'

'No,' she gasped her disbelief that he could still doubt it.

'Don't you know that uninterest is the surest way to induce interest?' he derided.

'Not you too!'

His eyes narrowed to steely slits. 'Someone else accused you of the same duplicity?'

'Your mistress!'

His mouth twisted without humour. 'Audra is well aware of the wiles of her own sex.'

Danielle's eyes flashed furiously, her control slipping fast. 'Except that this is no wile, and I have no interest in what either you *or* Miss McDonald think of me. Now let go of me!' she ordered through gritted teeth.

His head went back arrogantly. 'I'll let you go when I'm good and ready. And I'm not ready.' His head swooped and he took her lips in a savage kiss, ravaging her with little regard for the way she cringed away from him.

'Let go!'

'Like hell!' he bit out fiercely.

As he continued to kiss her, his tongue deeply plundering her mouth, Danielle was left with no will of her own, was drawn into Nick's desires for the second time in her life. And this time she hated every moment of it, felt a cold fury passing through her. She wouldn't be treated like just another woman he felt he could bed, she wouldn't!

She had tried to treat him like any other client, had intended being polite to him if nothing else, but he had made that impossible from the first, was intent now on punishing her for the fact that she didn't want him as he wanted her. But she had been punished enough in the past by this man, wasn't prepared to accept his cold-blooded arrogance for a second time.

As she wrenched away from him and saw the cold cruelty in his face, his satisfaction at forcing her to his will, she knew she had one weapon against him. After seven long years it was time to give him back his two hundred pounds—and the humiliation that had gone with earning it!

CHAPTER THREE

'WHERE did you two disappear to?' Lewis frowned in the darkness. 'Miss McDonald was furious!'

Danielle turned to look at him, Lewis driving her home from the club, the two of them leaving soon after she and Nick had returned to the table. 'I felt like some fresh air,' she invented. 'Miss McDonald was right, it was hot once you started dancing.'

He pulled a face. 'What you and Andracas were doing didn't look much like dancing to me!'

'Can you wonder I was hot?' she teased.

'Danielle——'

'Please, Lewis,' she sighed. 'I can do without you too.'

'What do you mean?' he raised dark blond brows.

'It's enough that Nick Andracas feels jealous of you, you don't have to feel the same way about him!'

Lewis frowned. 'Are you saying Andracas *is* attracted to you?' he sounded worried.

She repressed a shiver, still remembering the fury she had felt at being kissed against her will. 'Yes,' she answered flatly, her lack of enthusiasm obvious.

'But what about Miss McDonald?'

'She's his mistress.'

'But—I think this is all a little sophisticated for me,' Lewis looked uncomfortable.

'You're wrong, Lewis,' she told him sharply. 'It isn't sophisticated at all, it's very basic.'

51

He tried to look a little more blasé about the situation. 'Has he told you he's attracted to you?'

'Incessantly!'

'Then why did he look so angry when you both returned from the garden?'

Nick hadn't just been angry, he had been furious, making no secret of the fact, suggesting he and Audra leave immediately. After he had kissed her so contemptuously Danielle had made it clear to him that if he ever attempted to do it again she would see to it personally that some injury befell him.

She may have decided his despicable behaviour deserved retaliation this time, but she wasn't going to make any of this easy for him. She had been an easy conquest for him once before, she wasn't about to be so again, intended him to *feel* the humiliation of being bought when the time came.

'Use your imagination, Lewis,' she mocked him now.

His eyes widened. 'You really turned him down?' He didn't sound as if that were possible.

'Well of course I did,' she taunted his dismay. 'Have you forgotten I'm painting his mistress?'

'No. But——'

'Really, Lewis,' she lightly mocked. 'I'm shocked at this mercenary streak in you.'

He looked uncomfortable at the jibe. 'I just wouldn't like to upset an important client like him.'

'Did you hear him say anything about being upset?'

'No. . . .'

'Then don't worry so much,' she teased him. 'I can handle Mr Andracas.'

'I hope so.' But he didn't look very convinced by her confidence.

Danielle was very sure of that confidence, knew exactly what she was doing, and why.

She left her answering machine on the next day, not going to be available to Nick if he should happen to call. He didn't. She wasn't too surprised, knew that his will was as strong if not stronger than her own. But she also knew how determined he could be, that he didn't like to lose at anything he tried to do. He would approach her again, she felt sure of it.

Thursday turned out to be as unproductive where he was concerned, but still she didn't worry. This was a battle of wills, and after seven years of waiting for a revenge that had lain dormant in her until the moment he tried to take her for a fool a second time she felt she would be the victor in this particular battle. She had patience on her side for one thing, something Nick had shown he had little of.

Six telephone calls from him on Friday convinced her how right she was! All of them asked her to return his call, giving her the telephone number to do so, but she ignored every one of them. For once Nick Andracas was going to have to do more than click his fingers to get a woman to fall into bed with him. This particular woman anyway!

It was shortly before seven when someone pressed down impatiently on her doorbell and kept their finger there. Nick. She hadn't expected him to call personally quite so soon, but she wasn't worried by the visit, filled with a cool composure as she went to answer the door.

'Why the hell haven't you answered any of my

calls?' he demanded without preamble, his expression grim as he strode uninvited into her apartment.

'Calls?' she followed him, feigning innocence, but taking in the tailored brown suit and cream shirt he was wearing.

'Yes,' he rasped, turning to glower at her. 'I've telephoned you half a dozen times today.'

'I always leave my answering machine on while I'm working,' she shrugged. 'I haven't got round to listening to my messages yet today.'

'That isn't very efficient if someone needs to reach you urgently,' he said grimly.

She looked unconcerned by his vehemence, secretly elated that he was so upset. 'Most people call back,' she shrugged.

'I did,' he ground out. 'Five times!'

'As I told you, I haven't——'

'I heard you,' he cut in impatiently.

Danielle met his gaze coolly. 'Do you have new instructions for the portrait?' she pretended innocence at his reason for wanting to talk to her, although in reality the first of the messages had clearly invited her out to dinner this evening.

'Damn the portrait,' he predictably swore, his anger barely held in check. 'You know why I want to see you.'

'No——'

'Don't play games with me, Danielle,' his hands were clenched at his sides. 'Especially these sort of games. I don't participate very well.'

'And I don't like playing games,' her voice sharpened with displeasure. 'I thought we had settled this earlier in the week, Mr Andracas. Unless you wish to talk to me about the portrait or something pertaining to it I do not want to see you. Or hear from you,' she added pointedly.

He punched one clenched fist into the palm of the other hand. 'Stop pushing me, Danielle.'

'Pushing *you*?' she repeated incredulously. 'What you're doing to me amounts to harassment.'

'I want to see you, to be with you!'

'To go to bed with me,' she scorned hardly.

'That too if things worked out between us,' he acknowledged tautly.

'Don't treat me like an idiot, Nick,' she snapped. 'Bed is your prime objective.'

'And what's wrong with that?'

'Nothing. If I were willing. But I'm not,' she bit out with contempt.

'Do you have something against sex——'

'Don't throw that one at me!' she derided with a humourless laugh.

'You're driving me insane,' he ground out. 'I can't stop thinking about you.'

She didn't reveal the surge of elation she felt at this further admission. 'Talk to Miss McDonald about it, not me.'

His eyes narrowed. 'Does my relationship with Audra bother you?' he asked slowly.

She gave him a scornful look. 'Only in so far as I feel sorry for her.'

'You *what*?' he said in a hushed voice.

He was blazingly angry now, she could see that. And she was wary of it. Insulting him within the safety of other people was one thing, here they were too much alone, Nick too much of a threat. But she couldn't, wouldn't, withdraw her statement. 'You don't love her, Nick,' she derided. 'You're just using her until someone else comes along.'

His mouth twisted. 'Audra doesn't love me either. We have a—convenient arrangement.'

'And I'm trying to tell you that sort of arrangement wouldn't suit me at all!'

'You aren't giving me a chance!'

She almost choked at the injustice of that remark. He had had his chance with her seven years ago, he would never get another one. 'No,' she agreed tightly. 'Because I know it wouldn't work between us. Now if you'll excuse me, I'm going out in a few minutes.'

'With Vaughn?' he rasped.

'No, not with Lewis,' she met his gaze steadily, defying him to question her further.

'Another man?'

She thought of her promise to go to her parents' house tonight for her father's birthday. 'Yes,' she nodded.

'All right,' Nick bit out forcefully. 'If that's the way you want it.'

'It is,' she confirmed abruptly.

'I'm not going to ask you again,' he warned harshly, his expression grim.

'No,' she acknowledged mockingly without any real conviction as to it being true.

'I don't go around chasing women like this,' he added disgustedly, more to himself than to her.

She was sure he didn't, every woman he had ever wanted had been his for the choosing, even herself once. 'That's a welcome relief,' she taunted.

He looked more angry than ever. 'I wish I knew what it was about you that haunts me,' he muttered.

Her eyes widened. 'Haunts you?' she repeated in a soft voice. Surely he didn't recognise her as the girl he had once assumed was a prostitute and spent a few hours with?

He nodded grimly. 'You're beautiful, and yet not breathtakingly so. And yet I can't get the image of your corn-coloured hair and green eyes out of my mind. You're destroying me, Danielle.'

She knew her stubbornness in refusing to go out with him had angered him, but he was nowhere near being destroyed yet, because nothing penetrated the wall he had erected about his heart. And it was there that she wanted to reach him, wanted him to know the full pain of his own humiliation, as she had once done at his mercy.

'You don't give a damn, do you?' he realised softly.

She shrugged. 'I'm sure you'll get over it— probably when the next beautiful woman comes along.'

He gave a defeated sigh at her stubbornness, something she felt sure didn't happened to him very often. 'I'd better go, then.'

'Are you seeing Miss McDonald tonight?'

'None of your damned business,' he rasped.

Her brows rose mockingly. 'I just thought you might remind her of our two o'clock appointment tomorrow,' she said with saccharine sweetness.

'She'll be here,' he assured her arrogantly.

'Thank you,' she inclined her head in a mocking salute.

'Don't thank me,' his voice was harsh. 'The portrait is part of Audra's job.'

Despite Nick's arrogant assurance the actress was half an hour late the next day, and if her mood was anything to go by someone had already upset her today.

'I can only stay half an hour at the most,' she informed Danielle haughtily. 'I have a hairdressing appointment at three-thirty.'

Danielle shrugged her acceptance of the fact, not in a mood to be antagonised today. 'That just means we will have to have one more sitting than planned,' she said lightly. 'Would you like to go and change now?'

The actress seemed to take even longer doing that today too, leaving them only twenty minutes of the allotted half an hour. Not that Danielle minded, the less she had to do with the other woman the better.

'Have you seen Nick lately?'

Danielle took her time about answering the casually put question, knowing it was anything but, Audra's mouth tight. 'He called yesterday,' she dismissed.

The brown eyes glittered angrily. 'I thought you weren't interested in him!'

'I'm not.'

'Then——'

'Could you please sit still, Miss McDonald?' she requested with a sigh. 'We don't have much time today as it is,' she added pointedly.

The other woman stood up to pace the room. 'I suppose you think you've been very clever.'

'I do?' she sat back, realising that for now, at least, work was impossible.

Audra glared at her. 'I know you've been seeing Nick since Tuesday night,' she snapped.

She frowned, thinking the accusation through, not knowing what could have convinced the other woman of such a thing. 'Why do you think that?' she finally prompted.

'I know it,' the other woman's eyes glittered furiously.

'Then you know more than I do,' she shrugged.

Audra's mouth twisted into an ugly smile. 'I

know the two of you had been doing more than talking out on that balcony Tuesday night. I know how Nick looks when he's aroused.'

'You and a hundred other women!' Danielle heard herself make the bitchy comment as if in a dream.

'Why you——'

'I'm sorry,' she sighed. 'There's no point in the two of us resorting to insults. If you haven't seen Nick since Tuesday it certainly hasn't been because of me. He came here for about fifteen minutes last night, and you have to admit that isn't long enough for him to have even showered, let alone for the two of us to go to bed together,' she derided.

Audra looked uncertain. 'If you're lying to me. . . .'

'I'm not,' she answered steadily, although she wasn't sure she couldn't be the reason Nick hadn't seen his mistress since Tuesday. Maybe he really wanted her so much he could no longer feel any desire for the beautiful Audra? The thought filled her with triumph. Not too much longer now and he should be ripe for her revenge. Then she would see how the arrogantly cruel Nick Andracas liked his own humiliation.

She telephoned her mother once Audra had left, the two of them going shopping for an hour, her mother coming back to the apartment for a cup of tea before driving home.

'Your father has been a little concerned about you, dear,' she looked at Danielle anxiously.

She gave her a surprised look. 'I'm fine,' she assured her. 'You know I am.'

'You have been looking a little pale lately, a little like you did after——'

'Wrong time of the month,' she dismissed evasively, pouring their tea.

'But you looked pale last week too, Ellie,' her mother said concernedly, an older version of Danielle, the two of them having a wonderful rapport. Which wasn't always a good thing, especially at a time like this; it meant her mother knew her too well. 'You aren't working too hard?'

'Probably,' she smiled. 'But I'm definitely taking a holiday once this one is completed.'

'Can I see it?' her mother asked eagerly, both of her parents very proud of her work.

'Of course,' she took her mother through to the studio, a second bedroom that had been converted, one wall completely windows, as was most of the ceiling.

'It's marvellous, darling,' her mother enthused over the half-completed portrait. 'She's a very beautiful woman, isn't she?'

She had somehow managed to convey the other woman's outward beauty, the eyes, the mirrors of the soul, partly concealed by lowered lashes. It was the compromise Lewis had said she would find. 'Very beautiful,' she nodded.

'Doesn't she go out with that marvellous looking Greek man?' her mother asked vaguely as they returned to the lounge.

Danielle stiffened that her mother should mention Nick, although neither of her parents were aware of her involvement with him seven years ago. 'Nicholas Andracas,' she confirmed stiltedly. 'And he's more American than Greek.'

'You've met him, dear?'

'Briefly,' she evaded. 'As you said, he's a friend of Miss McDonald's.'

Her mother gave a coy smile. 'Rumour has it

they're a little more than that.'

'Mother,' she chided mockingly. 'And I never knew you were a gossip.'

'I'm not, Ellie,' she defended. 'But the man is notorious for his affairs.'

'Yes,' she acknowledged dully.

Her mother gave her a sharp look. 'You aren't attracted to him, darling?' she looked troubled by the thought.

She could understand her mother's worry if she were interested in Nick. Although her parents had never known the identity of her lover seven years ago they had both been aware of the way he had hurt her. 'No,' she answered with complete honesty, her feelings towards him completely opposite to attraction.

'You know we're only concerned for you, Ellie,' her mother explained gently. 'Nicholas Andracas is not the man for you. Now Lewis is a different matter . . .?'

She gave a throaty chuckle at her mother's attempt at matchmaking, both her parents having met and approved of Lewis. 'Actually he called this morning and invited me to a party,' she decided to give her mother this satisfaction if she couldn't give her anything else.

'And are you going?'

She laughed again at her mother's attempt not to look too enthusiastic about the news. 'Yes.'

'That's nice, dear.'

'Nice?' she teased.

'Lewis is a good man,' her mother defended her matchmaking. 'Steady and reliable.'

A shadow crossed over her face, leaving her eyes dark. 'He's very nice——'

'But boring,' her mother joked. 'I know. Still,

the party will make a pleasant change for you, won't it?'

After the disaster the evening had turned out to be the last time, she had felt she owed Lewis this date, had readily agreed when he telephoned and invited her out. Life was turning out to be a little complicated lately, the normality of Lewis's company was exactly what she needed.

It was quite late by the time her mother left, and after a hurried salad dinner she went into her bedroom to shower and change. She didn't know what it was that caught her attention about the green onyx jewellery box, but something told her it didn't look quite right, that it had been disturbed in some way. Her face paled as she moved towards it, her hands trembling slightly as she lifted the lid.

The two hundred pounds looked to be in the same position as usual, but it wasn't to that she went, putting it dismissively to one side to look at the miniature that lay beneath. As she had known it would be, it had been moved, was lying in a different position than the one she had left it in this morning. It was a likeness she had painted several years ago, was something that she looked at at the start of each day and again before she went to bed every night. The identity of the subject was unmistakable. And there could be only one person who could have looked in the jewellery box, only one person who would have such a devious interest in her things. What would Audra McDonald do with the knowledge she now had?

Lewis was as punctual as usual when he called for her later that evening, his gaze appreciative as he saw how beautiful she looked in the white gown, its halter-necked style suiting her tall elegance, her hair secured in a casual bun on top of her head, several tendrils falling loosely about her nape and ears.

'You look lovely,' he told her enthusiastically.

'So do you,' she smiled, liking his navy blue suit and lighter blue shirt.

He looked abashed, one of those men who felt uncomfortable taking compliments himself. 'Are you ready to leave?'

'Unless you want a drink first?' she offered.

'Not for me,' he refused.

'Then lead on MacDuff,' she instructed lightly, following him down to his car, determined that she wasn't going to worry for this one evening, especially after the shock she had received earlier. She had always felt uncomfortable about the other woman using her bedroom to change, although it hadn't occurred to her that Audra would actually invade her privacy in that way. 'There are two ground rules for tonight,' she told Lewis brittly.

'Oh?' he looked disappointed.

'Not those sort of rules,' she chided teasingly. 'Really, Lewis, I'm surprised at you.'

'I can't imagine why,' he grinned. 'I've made my feelings about you obvious since the first time we met.'

That was true, and she had been making it just as obvious ever since that she liked him only as a friend. 'All right, you can include no flirting with me too.' She laughed at his woebegone expression. 'You introduced the subject, Lewis,' she reminded.

'That's the trouble with me, I never know when to keep my mouth shut,' he grimaced. 'So what are these two rules?'

'Number one, I don't want to talk about work.'

'Neither do I, so that's easily settled.' He looked at her curiously as he waited for the second rule.

'Number two, I don't want to talk about Nick Andracas or anything remotely related to him. Also agreed?' she raised shaped brows over luminous green eyes.

'Well. . . .'

'Lewis!'

He grimaced. 'That might be a little more difficult,' he finally admitted ruefully.

'Why?' she demanded sharply.

'Well. . . . You see, I——'

He didn't need to explain any further, not any more. Danielle recognised the house in the exclusive part of London that he was parking the BMW outside, even though she had only seen it once before. The Andracas house!

'Lewis, who invited you to this party?' she turned to him stiltedly.

He looked evasive. I didn't think you would mind,' he almost pleaded. 'And I've heard he gives really good parties. I thought you would enjoy yourself. We don't have to stay long if you——'

'*When* did he invite you, Lewis?' she queried in a softly patient voice.

'He telephoned me this morning, just before I called you and asked you to come with me,' he told her reluctantly.

That's what she had thought! Well if Nick thought he had outwitted her he was mistaken. Forewarned is forearmed, and she was now fully armed. 'We had better go inside, then, hadn't we?' she said brightly, getting out of the car.

'Danielle——?' Lewis hastily followed her as she walked up the steps to the house.

'Hm?' she met his gaze with innocent inquiry.

He looked slightly overawed by her sudden composure. 'You aren't—angry or—anything?'

If she was it certainly wasn't at him; he didn't have a devious bone in his body. But she knew who did! 'Should I be?'

'Well—no. But——'

'Then I'm not,' she put her arm through the crook of his. 'We've been invited to a party, Lewis, so let's go and enjoy ourselves.'

He seemed relieved that she was taking it so well after telling him she didn't even want to talk about Nicholas Andracas, smiling his relaxation as they entered the house together.

Danielle wasn't relaxed at all, although that wasn't obvious from her smiling demeanour, looking at Nick with coolly uninterested eyes as he came over to greet them, the lounge much as she remembered it, filled to capacity with guests tonight, too.

'I'm so glad you could both make it,' he drawled, his gaze mocking on Danielle.

She met his gaze unflinchingly. 'I wouldn't have missed this for anything.'

'No?'

'No,' she echoed softly. 'Everyone has heard of the famous Andracas parties.'

'Indeed?' he didn't look impressed. 'Well I'm afraid there is only one Andracas here tonight. Will I do?'

'Er—Shall we go and get ourselves a drink, Danielle?' Lewis cut in before she could make the scathing reply that was imminent, wary of what she might say to this undoubtedly important man.

'Good idea, Vaughn,' Nick answered him. 'Carolyn, be a good girl and take Mr Vaughn over to the bar,' he requested of a beautiful blonde standing nearby.

'Oh, but——'

'Go ahead, Lewis,' Danielle smiled at him reassuringly. 'I'll see you in a few minutes.'

Nick's hand rested lightly on her waist as he guided her further into the room, and although she disliked the familiarity she raised no objection. 'I told you I wouldn't ask again,' he murmured close to her ear.

She looked up at him with emotionless eyes. 'So you asked Lewis instead,' she drawled.

He gave an inclination of his head in acknowledgment of his ploy. 'It worked too, didn't it,' he said with satisfaction.

'If by that you mean I came to your party with Lewis, then the answer is yes.' She moved pointedly away from him. 'But that's all your invitation has achieved. Where is Miss McDonald tonight?' she mocked.

Nick was more relaxed tonight on his own ground, the smoky grey velvet jacket fitting tautly across his shoulders, the black shirt and trousers moulded to the leanness of his body. 'She's here somewhere,' he dismissed. 'All the cast from the play are.'

Danielle frowned at his way of describing the other woman's presence here. 'I'd better go and find Lewis——'

His hand on her arm stopped her. 'He'll find us.'

'That isn't the point——'

'Audra and I are no longer seeing each other,' he held her gaze searchingly.

'But you just said——'

'She's here with the others, not as my personal guest.'

Danielle had had a strange feeling he was going to say that, had guessed it from the other woman's behaviour today, and the things she had said.

Obviously Nick now considered there were no barriers separating them but a little reluctance on her part—and no doubt he felt confident he could deal with that! 'I hope that isn't on my account,' she dismissed with uninterest. 'Because I came here with Lewis and I intend leaving with him.'

'A pity,' Nick drawled. 'I was hoping to persuade you not to leave at all.'

Her brows arched mockingly. 'Surely you don't entertain your lady friends here?'

'Usually they entertain me,' he told her with a taunting smile. 'But you're right, my family home is not usually the place for such friends. I have an apartment of my own near the park.'

'That's what I thought,' she said derisively, remembering the apartment well.

'But that wouldn't do for you,' he added with seductive softness.

'I'm different, hm?' she said with scepticism.

'Yes,' he ground out, angry at her derision. 'I want you for more than just——'

'Here we are.' Lewis had finally managed to push his way through the crowds of people in the room, the two glasses of champagne in his hands also intact. 'Sorry, Nick,' he gave him a rueful glance. 'I could only carry the two.'

Nick looked blazingly angry at the other man's success in frustrating his attempt to persuade Danielle into an affair with him. 'I'll talk to you both later,' he muttered, turning in the direction of the bar.

Lewis looked dazed by his behaviour. 'Did I say something?'

'Not a thing,' she assured him with a warm smile, determined the two of them would enjoy themselves, in spite of it being Nick Andracas' party.

Audra McDonald did not look as if she were exactly the life and soul of the party when Danielle caught a glimpse of her a short time later, listening with a bored expression to the efforts of the young Adonis at her side to gain her attention. Much as she disliked the other woman Danielle could not help feeling grudging respect for the fact that Audra had come here tonight despite the fact that Nick had discarded her so callously in the week.

When the two of them found themselves alone upstairs in one of the bathrooms later in the evening she could not help but feel wary, and not just because of the marked attention Nick had been paying her all evening.

Audra gave her a sideways glance as she retouched her lipgloss. 'I expected to see you here tonight,' she said conversationally.

'Really?' she brushed her hair. 'Then you knew a lot more than I did.'

'You just didn't listen to me before, did you, Danielle?'

'Sorry?'

'I won't lose Nick,' the other woman snapped, ready to leave the bathroom now.

She shrugged. 'I think you may already be too late to stop that happening.'

Brown eyes flashed the other woman's hatred of her. 'But I can so easily get him back again.'

'Then do so,' she invited, beginning to tense at the venomous gleam in the other woman's eyes.

'God, I could——' Audra unclenched her hands with effort. 'I want him back, Danielle,' she spoke in a calmer voice now. 'And if I have to I'll use what I saw this afternoon to do it.' She watched as Danielle paled, satisfaction in her expression. 'You know what I mean?'

'Yes, I know what you mean,' her voice was so soft it could barely be heard in the silence of the room.

'Then you'll give Nick up.' It was a statement rather than a question.

'He——' She started again. 'He isn't mine to give up,' she shook her head.

'Do your best,' Audra drawled, picking up her clutch-bag and leaving.

Danielle drew in a controlling breath. The other woman would carry out her threat if pushed to. And if she did that . . .!

CHAPTER FOUR

SHE couldn't sleep; *how* could she with the threat now hanging over her head? Much as she hated Nick and wanted to punish him for the past, she wanted to protect that past too. No matter how much Nick deserved to pay for his arrogance she would have to stay as far away from him as she could in future, or as far away as he would let her!

The ringing of the doorbell interrupted her pained thoughts, and she knew as she glanced at the clock at her bedside and saw it was two in the morning that her visitor could only be Nick Andracas—he was the only person she knew who would have the arrogance and nerve to wake someone up this time of morning!

She pulled on her négligé over her nightgown, going to the door. 'What do you want?' she hissed through the thickness of the wood.

'As I'm standing outside your apartment it must be obvious I want to speak to you,' he made no concessions to what time it was by lowering his own voice.

'You spoke to me—earlier.'

'Before you left so abruptly,' he acknowledged grimly. 'I want to know what Audra said to you.'

Poor Lewis, she had dragged him away from the party as soon as she could after Audra had made her threat, assuring him that Nick wouldn't notice their absence among so many other guests, not wanting to talk to him again when she was feeling so raw. She had been as wrong about under-estimating him as she had about the actress.

'I don't know what you're talking about,' she dismissed. 'Now if you don't mind, I'd like to go to bed. And shouldn't you be returning to your guests?' she added pointedly.

'My last guest left fifteen minutes ago,' he rasped. 'That's why I'm here.'

'*All* of your guests left?' she mocked. When she and Lewis had left so suddenly Audra had been leaning so close to Nick she was almost a part of him.

'All of them,' he confirmed abruptly. 'Now will you open this door and talk to me?'

'No.'

'Danielle——'

'I'm sorry,' she cut in sharply, knowing how close he was to losing his volcanic patience. 'But I don't intend opening this door to anyone this time of night.'

'You know it's me, damn you,' he ground out.

She could imagine the fury in his face, knew how he hated to be thwarted. 'Of course I know it's you,' she said softly. 'That's just another reason for not opening the door.'

The muffled swearing on the other side of the door told her that her barb had hit its mark. 'I'll be back, Danielle,' he warned her softly. 'And I don't intend leaving until I have some answers next time.'

She listened to the ascent of the lift as he waited for it, heard it go down again before she returned to her bedroom. Both of them knew that his threat where she was concerned was an idle one, that she didn't, and wouldn't, tell him anything she didn't want to. But Audra may not be so easy to handle. . . .

In the end she slept little, her sleep troubled
when she did manage to doze for a while, her
appearance heavy-eyed as she lingered over a pot
of coffee for her breakfast the next morning. She
had lived a relatively peaceful existence the last
seven years, and now within days of meeting Nick
again he was turning her world upside-down.

When she opened the door to him half an hour
later she wasn't exactly overjoyed to see him!

'I told you I would be back,' he walked into her
apartment uninvited, casually dressed in grey fitted
trousers and a navy blue shirt. 'Now tell me what
Audra said to make you leave last night,' he
pinpointed her with narrowed grey eyes, seeming
not to notice that she only wore her thin négligé
over her nightgown.

Danielle looked slightly to the left of his face,
unable to meet his gaze. 'I don't know what makes
you think Miss McDonald spoke to me at all,' she
dismissed lightly.

'Simple,' he drawled. 'She told me she had.'

'Oh,' Danielle paled slightly, wondering what
else the other woman told him. And then
dismissed the idea; if Audra had told him he
wouldn't need to ask.

'Yes,' he acknowledged grimly. 'She seemed to
think, for some reason, that I needed her help in
eliminating you from my life.' His expression
boded ill for the other woman.

For such an intelligent woman Audra McDonald
had been rather stupid in overestimating her, or
any other woman's, importance in Nick's life;
should have realised he would resent such
blatantly confessed interference. Or maybe the
other woman just felt confident enough of her 'ace
up her sleeve' to dare such a liberty. Whatever the

reason both women knew Danielle would never go out with Nick. Although that certainly didn't guarantee that he would go back to the other woman either, the opposite now, she would have thought.

'She still wants you,' she told Nick softly.

His mouth tightened. 'And we both know it's over between us,' he rasped.

'I think Miss McDonald would prefer it if it weren't,' she derided.

'I'm well aware of Audra's feelings in this,' he snapped. 'And now she's well aware of mine.'

That boded ill for Danielle, and she knew it, chewing worriedly on her inner lip. Audra certainly wasn't going to calmly sit back and take this.

'Go out with me just once, Danielle,' Nick's voice had softened persuasively. 'I promise you'll enjoy yourself,' he encouraged as she looked at him blankly, her thoughts far from his invitation.

But she had no doubt that he could be overwhelmingly charming if he wanted to be, she just couldn't go out with him, not now. 'I'm sorry,' she refused. 'Now if you'll excuse me,' she added pointedly. 'I'm going out.'

His mouth tightened ominously. 'With Vaughn?'

Until she had made the statement she had no intention of going out, now it seemed like a good idea. She couldn't sit here and brood all day, just wondering if Audra were going to use her knowledge against her. 'No, not with Lewis,' she answered evenly. 'I—I'm going to see my parents,' the idea suddenly occurred to her.

He frowned. 'Couldn't you see them some other time?'

'I could,' she nodded. 'But I told them I would go today, and I always keep my promises.'

'Danielle——'

'I have to leave in a few minutes,' she cut in firmly. 'So if you wouldn't mind . . .?'

'But I do mind,' he grated. 'Why the hell won't you just go out with me?'

She shrugged. 'Just look at the fate that befell Miss McDonald and you'll know,' she derided.

Colour darkened his cheeks. 'I never promised her forever,' he rasped.

'You never promise any woman that,' she taunted. 'Only here and now, and enjoying yourselves while you can.'

'And what's wrong with that?'

'Nothing—for you.'

His mouth twisted. 'You want a white gown and a gold wedding ring, hmm?' he scorned.

Her eyes flashed deeply green. 'I want a man I can love and respect, and not necessarily in that order.' She gave him a scathing look. 'Do you think you fit the description?'

His expression was glacial, 'I know I don't,' he bit out.

'Then you have your answer,' she shrugged, going into her bedroom, leaving it his decision to leave.

She may have appeared calm while she was talking to Nick but this was the least calm she had ever felt, leaning weakly against the door. How could she have once loved such a man so much she had given herself to him at their first meeting? How could she *still* feel that trembling of awareness where he was concerned?

She hadn't believed she could feel that way about him after all this time, hadn't felt that way about any man for the last seven years. Certainly no one could accuse her of being promiscuous, she thought hysterically. In all of her twenty-six years she had known only one lover, and he had treated her cruelly enough for her never to want another!

Then why was she so physically aware of him? All the time she had been talking to him this morning she had been conscious of how ruggedly handsome he was, of how the blue shirt and grey trousers moulded to the lean length of his body, had remembered the beauty of that body and the ecstasy it had once given her, if only briefly.

A shower made her feel a little better, and she dressed in a cool lime-green sundress with tiny ribbon straps, a fitted bodice, and loose skirt, needing the look of femininity to bolster her sadly flagging self-confidence, her hair fresh and golden, her only make-up a peach lipgloss. She looked young and attractive, showing none of her confusion of a few minutes ago, she dismissed the intimate thoughts from her mind.

Nick stood up as she entered the lounge, his gaze appreciative on her young loveliness. 'It was worth waiting for,' he murmured softly.

'I thought you would have gone by now,' she snapped ungraciously, the image of cool confidence at once crumbling, leaving her strangely vulnerable when she wanted to be strong.

He shrugged unconcernedly. 'I thought I could drive you to your parents' home.'

And check that she was actually going there! 'I can drive myself,' she picked up her car keys pointedly. 'In fact, I would prefer to do so. That way I have a lift home again.'

He gave an inclination of his head in acknowledgment of her decision. 'Then I'll walk you to your car.' He took a firm hold of her arm.

'That isn't necessary,' she snapped, trying to free herself and failing miserably.

'I'm leaving anyway,' he pointed out reasonably.

If only she didn't feel so *un*reasonable when in his company! In fact, she could feel positively violent at times when he was around. Especially times like this, feeling herself guided firmly in the direction of the lift, whether she wanted to go or not.

'You see, I didn't,' he drawled mockingly as they stepped out into the sunshine.

She blinked up at him, had been lost in her own thoughts the last few minutes. 'Didn't what?'

He gave a wolfish smile. 'Ravish you in the lift,' he taunted throatily.

Her face paled as she vividly remembered a time he *had* made love to her in a lift.

'Hey?' all humour left him as he gently clasped her arms, looking down at her concerned. 'What is it?'

'I——'

'Look this way, Mr Andracas,' a voice called out cheerfully from behind them.

They both turned simultaneously, and as they did so a camera clicked, Nick's arm going about her protectively as the camera clicked again.

'Thanks, Mr Andracas, Miss Smith,' the reporter grinned cheekily, a man in his mid-thirties, weighed down by the trappings of his profession. He turned quickly to get into a waiting car.

Danielle was suddenly galvanised into action. 'Hey, stop——'

'Leave it,' Nick rasped at her side, his hands tightening on her arms as the car drove away.

'But——'

'All you'll do by chasing after him is add to his story,' he pointed out resignedly. ' "Latest

Andracas mistress denies romance",' he quoted
with a sigh.

Danielle wrenched out of his grasp. 'Because
there isn't,' she said forcefully.

'A denial will only increase their speculation,' he
reasoned. 'The fact that I'm leaving your
apartment with you now gives the impression I
spent the night here.'

'But you didn't!' she gasped.

He gave her a pitying glance. 'And who do you
think will believe that?'

'Anyone who knows me!'

'And everyone else, the people who know *me*?'
he pointed out mockingly.

She looked at him with hate in her eyes, tears
glistening there. 'God, how I despise you,' she told
him vehemently. 'I despise everything about you.
But especially this. I'll never forgive you for it.
Never!'

'Danielle——'

'Don't touch me,' she evaded his reaching grasp.
'You probably arranged all this just to compromise
me into going out with you!' she added accusingly.

He shook his head. 'Don't be ridiculous. I hate
this sort of publicity as much as the next man.'

'Then how would that reporter have known to
come to *my* apartment?' she scorned.

Nick shrugged, sighing deeply. 'He could have
followed me——'

'Or he could have been told precisely where you
would be,' she finished pointedly.

'Not by me,' he grated.

'And certainly not by me,' she snapped.

His mouth thinned. 'That leaves only one
person who could have even guessed I would be
coming to see you today. Audra!'

Danielle's eyes widened as he rasped the other woman's name. It would be the sort of thing the other woman would do, but that didn't mean that she had. Although someone had directed that reporter to her apartment. 'I don't care *who* it was,' she told Nick sharply. 'I just don't want to be caught up in your publicity ever again!' She turned on her heel and walked over to her parked car.

'Danielle. . . .'

She turned to look at him briefly before getting into her car, the sunlight giving his hair an ebony sheen. 'Yes?'

'Have a nice day?' he called softly.

She gave a snort of disgust before climbing into her car, watching as he swung lithely inside the sleek Ferrari parked at the roadside, the black model of the past replaced by this silver one. He drove past her with a brief wave of acknowledgment.

Danielle drove more slowly than him, giving herself time to think, intending to go to her parents' house now that she was out of the apartment.

Nick had been adamant that he had had nothing to do with the reporter being outside her apartment, and she believed him. He knew her well enough by now to know how she would react to such publicity, how she liked to keep a low profile. That only left Audra and the threat she had made yesterday evening. The reporter trailing her and Nick was another warning; she had a feeling things could get a lot rougher.

God, how she wished she had followed her instincts that day Lewis brought her this latest commission, wished she had refused it and stayed as far away from Nick as she could. If she weren't careful he would destroy her life a second time, and there wouldn't be a thing she could do to stop it.

Her parents were pleased, if surprised, to see her again so soon after she had spent the evening with them on Friday, and she saw her father giving her several probing glances. Tall, and still handsome in his mid-fifties, her father hardly looked the part of the successful businessman he was, people who didn't know him personally often mistaking him for one of his own accountants. But he could be ruthless if the occasion merited it, and where his family was concerned he fiercely guarded his own.

'Your mother is worried about you,' he was looking at her closely.

The two of them sat together in the garden of her parents' Richmond home, her mother just having gone into the house to check on when the lunch would be ready. 'That's strange,' Danielle gave him a teasing smile. 'Mummy said the same thing about you when we went shopping yesterday.'

He pulled a face. 'I forget how astute you are. All right,' he nodded. 'We're both concerned about you. Your mother tells me you've become involved with Nick Andracas.'

Danielle relaxed back in the garden chair, at ease now that she was with her family. 'I'm sure Mummy didn't tell you any such thing,' she sipped her sherry. 'I've already explained to her that he's just a client of mine.'

'Hm, well I don't think it's a good idea for you to have met him at all.'

'Why?'

'I know the sort of man he is,' her father looked

grim. 'He always wants what he can't have, and that includes women as well as business.'

Danielle frowned at this correct description of Nick. 'I didn't realise you knew him?'

'I don't, at least, not personally. He tried to take over my company a couple of years ago, and he didn't mind what he paid to get it.'

'I didn't realise that,' she said dazedly.

'No, well I don't like to bother you and your mother with business. But I haven't been unaware of the relatively solitary existence you've lived in recent years,' he told her softly. 'And to a man like Andracas you would be a tremendous challenge.'

'I'm not interested,' she dismissed.

'I wasn't interested in selling either,' he said ruefully. 'But he damn nearly got me. I don't want to interfere in your life, Ellie, I just don't want you hurt again.'

'I know that,' she touched his arm gratefully. 'And I can assure you, I won't be.'

Which was easy to say, but she still remembered the awareness she had felt very briefly this morning. It had been a definite sexual awareness, one she had thought never to feel again, one she didn't want to feel again. Her father was right, Nick was a very dangerous man.

He was also waiting for her when she got back to her apartment later that afternoon! And from the look of him he had been waiting some time.

'I know, I know,' he held up his hands defensively as he climbed out of the car and came towards her. 'You don't want to see me here again. But I thought I should let you know that I tracked down the reporter that was here this morning. I've been waiting over an hour,' he cajoled.

Her eyes widened that he had taken the trouble to look for the other man after telling her it wasn't worth it. 'You had better come upstairs.'

'Don't worry,' Nick taunted at her lack of enthusiasm for the idea. 'He isn't here now, lurking behind a car or something.'

She gave him a scathing glance. 'You had better come up anyway.'

He was still wearing the same clothes he had had on that morning, the shirt now a little damp against his back in the heat of the day. Danielle felt the frisson of awareness down her spine once again.

She faced him across the room once they had entered her apartment. 'What did the reporter say?'

Nick had sprawled himself in one of her armchairs, looking relaxed and at home. 'He works freelance, and had already sold the story and photograph by the time I found him,' he grimaced.

Danielle paled a little. 'Do you have any idea what the article will say?'

He shrugged. 'The usual trash, I would imagine.'

She gave a deep sigh. 'Thank you for taking the time to let me know,' she said dully.

'Hey, look, I really am sorry,' he sat forward in the chair. 'I offered to buy the story off him myself, but I was just too late. And the newspaper, as you can imagine, just didn't want to know.'

'Which one is it?'

He named one of the more gossipy daily newspapers. 'They'll be printing it tomorrow,' he revealed reluctantly as he saw how upset she was.

She nodded. 'Thank you for trying, anyway.'

He shrugged. 'Don't thank me, I couldn't do a thing, except probably make things worse, as I warned you it would. I don't suppose you feel like making me a sandwich, do you?' he looked at her encouragingly. 'I didn't have time for lunch running around after the reporter.'

The logic in her told her to say no, to tell him to go to his own home and get something to eat. And yet he *had* chased around London trying to stop the reporter selling his story. A sandwich wasn't a high price to pay for that, even if he hadn't succeeded. 'I'll get you something,' she moved towards the kitchen, glancing back to find him immersed in the Sunday newspaper.

He looked so completely at home in her lounge, as if he spent a lot of his time there. She was mad to have agreed to getting him something to eat!

In the end she shared the chicken salad with him that she had meant for her own dinner, bread something she rarely bought, which meant she couldn't make him a sandwich. It was very unnerving sitting down to eat with him, gave a normality to their relationship that she would rather hadn't been there. The way they had met in the past, Nick picking her up at a party and then casually sleeping with her was how she wanted to think of him; eating dinner together made Nick seem human, when she knew he was inhuman.

'You can even make coffee,' he appreciatively drank the last of his creamless sugarless brew. 'You're a woman of many talents, Danielle Smith,' he smiled at her, a warmly intimate smile.

'Miss McDonald doesn't cook?'

'I never asked,' he derided. 'But I know my ex-wife couldn't even open a can.'

It was the first time she had heard him refer to

Beverley since the night seven years ago when he had spoken of her so bitterly. He didn't seem bitter now. 'Can you?' she derided.

He looked scandalised at the question. 'I'm Greek, remember?' he mocked. 'Mama made sure all her children could cook—and not out of a can either.'

'How many children are there?' she was curious in spite of herself.

'Six,' he grinned at her wide-eyed look. 'Five girls, and only one boy.'

Her mouth quirked with humour. 'Which means you were a spoilt little boy too.'

'Too?'

'You're definitely a spoilt big boy,' she mocked.

Nick chuckled softly. 'Mama didn't believe in spoiling children, I had to do my share of the chores. Although with so many of us it wasn't too bad.'

She turned away, realising how easily she was succumbing to his charm. 'I'm an only child. I wouldn't know.'

'That's a pity. For you, I mean.'

'What you don't have you never missed,' she shrugged. 'You have no children of your own?' she asked the question, but she already knew the answer. He and Beverley had been childless.

His mouth firmed. 'I have dozens of nieces and nephews, ranging from all ages.'

'I can imagine you have, but it isn't the same as children of your own, is it?'

He shrugged. 'I doubt I would make a very good father, anyway. You could hardly have a spoilt father *and* a spoilt child,' he said self-derisively. 'Is there any more coffee?' he abruptly changed the subject.

Danielle moved to get it for him, deep in thought as she went into the kitchen. He spoke so dismissively about children of his own, and yet she sensed a steel edge beneath the lightness of his voice, a pain he didn't want to talk about. And she disagreed with him about the sort of father he would make, knew he would be firm but loving with his children, as most Greek men were.

He was standing over by the window when she came back into the lounge, the broadness of his back a tautly rigid line. As she watched him, Nick unaware of her presence for the moment, he ran a weary hand around the back of his nape.

'Your coffee,' she broke the moment of intimacy, not wanting to feel any compassion for a man who had never felt any for anyone else, who lived his life to suit himself and didn't give a damn about others. 'And then I'm afraid you'll have to go,' she told him stiltedly. 'I intend working this evening.'

'It's all right, Danielle,' his mouth twisted into the facsimile of a smile. 'I won't overstay my welcome.'

He had done that the moment he arrived; she should never have invited him in. 'Perhaps after you've drunk your coffee . . .? I don't wish to seem rude——'

'But you're going to be anyway,' he grinned good naturedly, taking the coffee and swallowing it in one gulp even though it must have been very hot. 'Thank you for dinner, Danielle, I enjoyed it.'

Her own enthusiasm for their time spent together was noticeably absent. But she couldn't help it, couldn't lie even for politeness' sake. She wanted him out of here, and as quickly as possible, the last couple of hours a complete strain to her, even if they had passed quite quickly.

'Walk me to the door,' he quirked his brows encouragingly.

'It's just across the room,' she said dryly.

'Humour me, hm?' his eyes were a warm compelling grey.

With a rueful shrug she followed him over to the door, unprepared for the way his head bent and he claimed her mouth in a piercingly intense kiss. She had been out with several men since that night with Nick, had even enjoyed their kisses, but none of them had ever affected her as deeply, or spontaneously, as Nick was doing now.

He stepped back, no triumph in his eyes at the response he must have known he evoked, just a warm glow in the often cruelly assessing eyes. 'Don't work too hard,' he touched her cheek with gentle fingertips.

'Work . . .? Oh—oh yes.' She knew she wouldn't be able to work tonight, not now. 'I mean no!'

Nick smiled at her total confusion. 'I'll come round and see you tomorrow.'

'No!'

'Yes,' he insisted softly, his steely gaze compelling her to agree.

She turned away. 'I work during the day——'

'So do I now,' he drawled mockingly, smiling as her eyes widened in surprise. 'I decided to take notice of your advice——'

'*My* advice?' she echoed in an astounded voice, unable to remember ever advising this man about *anything*.

He nodded, enjoying her confusion. 'Just over a week ago you pointed out that I'm bored with my life——'

'Only because you pushed me into saying it!' she defended indignantly.

'Why you said it isn't important,' he dismissed. 'That fact that you did, and that it's the truth, is. As of tomorrow I've decided to be more than just a figurehead to my little empire, to take back the reins of power that I gave up several years ago,' the last came out grimly.

'I'm sure the business world is quaking in its shoes,' she said dryly, remembering how ruthless her father had said he found Nick to deal with in the past.

His mouth quirked. 'Not quite yet,' he drawled. 'But they will be,' he predicted.

She could believe that, although it was a little difficult to believe a scathing remark she had made had effected this change in him. And she said so.

Nick shrugged. 'The move has been coming about for some time. Being rich and idle is boring, in fact just being idle is, no matter how much money you have or don't have. The fact that you don't like my lifestyle did come into it, though. You've made your contempt for my image obvious, so I'm cleaning it up.'

'I doubt it will make any difference to me,' she told him honestly, shaking her head.

'Maybe not,' he accepted. 'But having a purpose in life again *will* make a difference to me. Cheer up, Danielle,' he mocked her frowning expression. 'You've done me a favour even if you won't go out with me.'

For the first time she realised that he was different today, that the bitterness she had known in him in the past, the cynical derision about everyone and everything that she had come to expect from him, were no longer there, that they had been replaced with a lighter, less grim Nick, one who no longer ordered with that familiar arrogance, but cajoled and teased instead. She wasn't sure she was up to handling this new Nick, didn't completely understand him. It also made it difficult for her to continue hating him when he was no longer the cold man of the past.

'Why give it all up in the first place if you're looking forward to returning to it so much?' she asked stiltedly.

His mouth thinned. 'I had my reasons at the time. But they seem less important now,' he shrugged off those reasons. 'I'm not sure what time I'll get here tomorrow——'

'I'd rather you——'

'Didn't come at all,' he finished softly. 'I know. But tonight wasn't so bad, was it?'

Besides the fact that she found being alone with him like this unnerving, the evening had been quite a pleasant one. And that was what she was afraid of!

'If you won't go out with me then I'll stay in with you,' he didn't wait for her reply. 'And tomorrow I'll bring the food and the wine.'

'But——'

'Now don't get in a panic, Danielle,' he mocked. 'It's only a meal and a chat, like tonight. I'll see you tomorrow,' he touched her cheek once more before leaving.

Danielle was left feeling as if she had been hit by a car travelling at high speed; as if she had been bulldozed down in its path! She had been wrong about Nick, the arrogance was still very much there, although heavily concealed by the sudden charm.

What she was going to do about him she didn't know, he still wouldn't take no for an answer!

The article and photograph of them together the

next morning in the newspaper made her wish more than ever that he weren't coming back to her apartment tonight. The photograph was very deceptive, making it look as if she were in Nick's arms instead of being protected from the photographer by him, her face buried against his chest. They had the look of two lovers who couldn't stop touching each other!

And the article written with it was even more damning, stating that Nick had arrived in the early hours of the morning and that the photograph showed the two of them leaving together the next day. This was exactly the sort of innuendo and suggestion this newspaper specialised in, lying by omission. If the reporter had seen Nick arrive at her apartment at two o'clock in the morning then he must also have seen him leave again a few minutes later, as he must have seen him arrive again shortly before ten. The article implied they had spent the evening and night together. And as Nick had predicted, his efforts to get the story stopped had only added to their speculation of how serious the relationship was.

It was exactly the fuel Audra McDonald needed to reveal her vindictive secret. And Danielle had a feeling she would do so very shortly.

She went to the onyx jewellery box, taking out the miniature to hold it to her protectively.

CHAPTER FIVE

By the time Nick arrived at seven that evening Danielle had experienced one of the worst days of her life. Several more reporters had tried to get in to talk to her, although she had refused to comment to any of them, slamming the door in the face of the reporter she recognised from yesterday before he even had time to say anything. Her father had telephoned to make sure she was all right, and although he didn't question her about the previous night she told him the true version anyway. And lastly, and worst of all, she hadn't been able to contact Audra McDonald.

She had telephoned the theatre where the actress was rehearsing for her play, had called her home too, and the reply as always the same, Miss McDonald was unavailable. She had even left a message for the other woman to call *her*. The return call had never come.

Nick frowned as he saw how pale she looked, putting the two bags of food that he carried in the kitchen before coming back to study her closely. 'That bad, hm?' he murmured regretfully.

She blinked darkened lashes over shadowed green eyes, hadn't made any effort to change out of the fitted denims and cream camisole top she had worn all day. 'Sorry?'

'You've had a lousy day,' he stated with a sigh, clasping her arms to sit her down in one of the armchairs. 'The press have been hounding you?' he looked down at her with narrowed eyes.

He spoke like one who knew what it felt like.
'They came to see you too?'

'They tried,' his mouth twisted. 'I have a little
more protection from such people than you do.'

She looked down at her hands, clean of the
paint today that usually spotted them, too
disturbed to work today, especially on Audra's
portrait. 'You saw the article they wrote?'

'Yes,' he grimaced his distaste for such trashy
writing. 'It was worse than even I imagined.'

'Yes,' Danielle acknowledged dully.

'I've also seen Audra,' his eyes were hard as he
spoke of the other woman.

Danielle's panicked gaze flew to his harsh face,
swallowing hard as she saw there was no accusation
in his eyes for her, only anger at the other woman.
Audra couldn't have told him, not yet anyway. 'I
tried to reach her on the telephone today,' she
revealed flatly. 'She refused to talk to me.'

His mouth twisted with grim humour. 'When
you're her backer you tend to get better results.'

'What did she say?'

'What could she say?' he shrugged, pacing the
room, the brown trousers moulded to his thighs
and legs, the cream of his shirt emphasising the
swarthiness of his skin. 'She set that particular
hound on us, she couldn't and didn't, deny that.'

But it seemed that Audra hadn't told him a lot
else. What was the actress waiting for? Was she
delaying telling Nick about her?

'She won't do that again,' he added harshly.
'Not if she wants to continue in this play.'

Danielle moistened suddenly dry lips. 'You—
threatened her?'

'I warned her,' he amended hardly.

It amounted to the same thing, and she knew

the other woman wouldn't have liked that one little bit. God, Danielle felt ill at what the actress could do to her, wanted to hide herself away until it was all over. But Nick had other ideas!

'I'll go and make our dinner while you sip a glass of wine,' he decided.

'I don't——'

'Forget about Audra's vindictiveness, Danielle,' he instructed from the kitchen doorway. 'She's vented her spite on me now, there's nothing else she can do.'

If only that were true! Danielle obediently sipped the wine he brought her a few seconds later, could hear him moving about her kitchen preparing their meal, too numb to stop him, realising as she smelt the food cooking that she was hungry, having forgotten to eat all day.

There was a thick soup to start accompanied by French bread, followed by a tasty meat dish that Nick assured her was his mother's secret recipe. 'She only confided it to people she really liked,' he added softly. 'I have a feeling she would have liked you, Danielle.'

Colour entered her cheeks at his blatant flirting with her. 'She's dead?' Danielle felt a little more relaxed after the delicious meal he had prepared for her, although she was still pale.

Nick nodded. 'Several years ago. My father too. Let's take our coffee through to the lounge and talk there,' he suggested softly. 'Unless you want some more food?' he indicated the cheese neither of them had touched.

'No, thank you,' she followed him through to the other room, sipping the strong coffee he had made them. 'Were you close to your parents?'

'Very,' he nodded.

'I suppose being the only boy they expected a lot from you,' she nodded.

His gaze sharpened. 'What do you mean?'

She looked taken aback by his sudden abruptness after the lazy charm he had displayed throughout the meal. 'Only that your career as head of the Andracas empire must have been a foregone conclusion,' she explained in a puzzled voice.

'Oh. I see,' he bit out. 'Yes, I suppose it was,' he visibly relaxed. 'But I never resented it.'

'Not many people would,' she mocked.

He gave a slight smile. 'I enjoyed walking in there today, especially seeing the expressions on the faces of my directors when they realised I wasn't just making my usual fleeting visit,' he added with relish. 'They all began to look guilty of something even though they weren't.'

'Maybe they are,' she taunted. 'Maybe they've all been embezzling off you for years.'

'Danielle,' he spoke in a humouring tone. 'I may not have been at my office every day but I can assure you I've known exactly what was going on in my company.'

She could tell that he had too, that even the playboy image she had accused him of had been a false one, that Nick Andracas would never be taken for a fool in any capacity, no matter how he seemed to treat life as a continual playground.

'What sort of music do you like?' with another one of his lightning changes of mood he strode across the room to look at her record collection. 'Everything from Brahms to Duran Duran,' he said admiringly. 'Hm, I think we'll put this one on.'

Danielle instantly recognised the LP cover as belonging to a collection of 10c.c. love songs. 'I've appreciated your being here tonight, and making me dinner,' she spoke quickly. 'But it's getting late now, and——'

'It's ten o'clock,' he mocked as he put the LP on the stereo before standing up. 'Even for you that has to be early.' He came across the room to sit beside her on the sofa.

She was at once aware of how dangerous this situation had become, that her need earlier for a little sympathetic company could lead to disaster. 'I think you had better go——'

'And if I don't want to,' long fingers caressingly touched the hair at her nape.

'This is my home, so it isn't your choice,' she told him stiffly.

'What are you afraid of?'

'Nothing,' she snapped, knowing that at this moment she was frightened of—*everything*.

'You're a liar,' his voice was husky against her ear. 'I won't hurt you, Danielle.'

She almost choked at the irony of that statement. Seven years ago she had been a light-hearted teenager, that had changed the moment she met Nick, and she hadn't known a day's real happiness in all the years since then. 'Didn't you read all of the article?' she scorned. 'According to them I don't have a heart to hurt.' Somehow the newspaper had managed to find one of the few men she had been out with the last few years, and he had told them how cold she was, how unemotional. 'They seem to think we're very well matched,' she added with brittle humour, knowing how untrue that was. This man had never had a heart to break, whereas hers had once broken into a thousand pieces. Was it any wonder it couldn't be put back together again?

'That man, the one they asked about you,' Nick was so close now his breath warmed her throat. 'Was he your lover?'

She gave him a pitying glance. 'Isn't the answer to that obvious?' she derided.

'The man was talking out of spite,' Nick guessed, 'because you turned him down.'

'Yes.'

'Have you ever had a lover?'

She stiffened at the question. 'Of course,' she rasped tightly. 'This is the time of lovers and not commitment. I wouldn't like to be unfashionable,' she added with bitterness.

'Then why——'

'We've had this conversation before, Mr Andracas, many times,' she cut in with a sigh. 'And my answer is still the same, even if you have tried to clean up your image,' she mocked.

His mouth quirked at her humour. 'I have to admit that resuming control of my company was as much for my benefit as impressing you,' he drawled.

'More so,' she taunted, aware that the wine and sweet music were acting like a narcotic on her senses, that her denial a few minutes ago of wanting an affair with him had lacked conviction. 'Nick, I think you should——'

'So do I,' he murmured throatily, moving closer, his body warm against hers.

'No, not that——!' She tried to push him away as his lips grazed her throat before his teeth bit gently into her earlobe. 'Please, not that . . .!' she groaned weakly, a fierce longing enveloping her as she turned into his arms. 'Oh, Nick,' she melted against him with a feeling like coming home after being away for a very long time.

He took the gift of her mouth with a gentleness that reached into her bones, her lips parting to deepen the kiss, fire coursing through her as his tongue moved warmly into her mouth to probe and caress the moist erotica he found there. Like a flower that had been denied sustenance too long she opened up to him, quivering uncontrollably as his hand closed over her breast, the hardened peak of her nipple clearly discernible through the soft material of her camisole.

'How long has it been for you?' Nick groaned at her instant response to his caresses.

'Too long!' She shuddered in reaction as he pushed the camisole above her bare breasts, bending his head to put his mouth against one taut peak, taking the nipple fully into his parted lips as she arched against him, alternately kissing the rosy tip with his moist tongue before biting down on the sensitive nub, loving the feel of her trembling beneath him.

Danielle had no control over her reaction now, could only hold on tightly to the broadness of his shoulders as he transferred his attention to the other breast, her head thrown back as she writhed beneath him in spasms of pleasure so acute she thought she might explode with the sheer ecstasy of it.

She did exactly that as his hand moved to the mound beneath her denims, her eyes wide as pleasure wracked through her body like an exquisite flame.

She clung tightly to him as the spinning began to steady, as a warm lethargy settled over her body after such mindless ecstasy had claimed it, her face buried against his chest as he cradled her to him. 'I'm sorry,' she choked her shame over what had just happened. 'I'm so *sorry!*' she groaned.

'It was beautiful, Danielle,' his voice was gruff, his arms like steel bands about her, as if he feared she might try to escape him. 'Anything that pleasures you couldn't help but be.'

'No, it was selfish. It was——'

'Wonderful,' he insisted gently. 'No passion between two people can ever be called selfish.'

'But you didn't—Only I——'

'This time,' he nodded, his eyes a velvety grey at her embarrassed confusion. 'This time was for you. But next time——'

'No!' she shook her head in sharp denial, pushing out of his arms. 'There must never be a "next time".' She looked up at him with horror for what she had just allowed to happen.

'Danielle——'

'No, please,' she evaded his arms, standing up, swaying in the aftermath of her passion. 'This should never have happened——'

'But it did,' he pointed out gently, looking at her with narrowed eyes, his dark hair ruffled. 'And I'm never going to forget that it did.'

It was completely the wrong thing to say in the circumstances; he had once forgotten her all to. easily! 'I want you to go now,' she told him stiltedly.

'Danielle, don't——'

'Please!'

He gave a deep sigh, standing up slowly, his eyes still showing the depth of his own arousal. 'Don't hate me for what I just did, Danielle,' he pleaded softly.

'Hate *you?*' she said with self-disgust. 'I was the one who lost control.'

'But you didn't do it alone,' he soothed gently. 'I wanted to give you that pleasure.'

Yes, it had been Nick's caresses that drove her to such wild abandon, as only his caresses ever had. But that only made her feel worse. What was happening to the hate she had had for him for so long, how *could* she hate a man and still feel such pleasure when in his arms? She was full of self-loathing for what she had done, for the ecstasy she had let Nick give her.

'Get a good night's sleep, Danielle,' he encouraged throatily. 'I'll see you tomorrow.'

There was no point in saying no, Nick Andracas was a law unto himself, and he would do exactly as he pleased. She felt his lips against her forehead with numbed acceptance, hearing the door to her apartment close softly a few seconds later.

The sobs wracked through her body in fierce remorse as she fell weakly on to the sofa, crying until she had no more tears left, the sobs still shuddering through her body. She had sworn to herself that Nick would never make love to her again, and tonight she had broken that promise all too easily. She hated herself as much as she hated him!

The ringing of the telephone woke her the next morning, and she stumbled from her bed to answer it with a feeling of not being quite awake, as her father seemed to make no sense on the other end of the line.

'You'll have to talk slower and more calmly,' she finally interrupted him. 'I don't understand what you're saying.'

For a moment there was silence, then, 'Have you seen a newspaper this morning?' he probed gently.

She frowned groggily. 'I've only just got out of bed, your call woke me.'

'Oh God . . .!' he groaned. 'Darling, I'm coming over.'

'Now?'

'Right now!'

The last remnants of sleep left her at the deep concern in his voice. 'Daddy, what is it? What's happened?' Panic began to engulf her.

'I'll be there as soon as I can,' he promised before ringing off abruptly.

Danielle felt a terrible sense of forboding assail her. What could the newspapers have printed that had so disturbed her father? Could a reporter have possibly been lurking about outside her apartment last night as Nick left?

She was showered and dressed by the time her father rang the doorbell fifteen minutes later, shocked at how grey and drawn he was. 'Daddy, what——'

'Sit down, Ellie,' he instructed firmly, striding over to her drinks cabinet to pour out a large measure of brandy.

Danielle had sat as soon as he told her to, but her eyes widened at his second move. 'Isn't it a little early in the day for you, Daddy?' she prompted in a concerned voice.

'It isn't for me,' he held the glass out in front of her. 'It's for you.'

'Me . . .?'

'Believe me, darling,' he said grimly. 'You're going to need it.'

She continued to frown, taking the glass with shaking fingers. 'Is it really that bad?' she attempted lightness.

'Just drink the brandy, Ellie,' he encouraged softly. 'Then we'll talk.'

She swallowed a little of the brandy, feeling its

warmth hit her empty stomach, briefly wondering what it would make of its unusual breakfast this morning. 'All right, Daddy,' she looked up at him unflinchingly. 'I'm ready now for whatever it is you want to tell me.'

'I don't want to tell you, Ellie,' he told her regretfully. 'But someone has to break the news, and I think it should be one of the family.'

'Mummy——'

'Is safely at home.' He took a newspaper out of his jacket pocket. 'Look at this, darling, and—and just remember that your mother and I were here for you then and we're here for you now, that we always will be.'

His assurance only made her trepidation grow, and as she unfolded the newspaper she saw the reason for his obvious concern. The headline read, 'Latest Andracas girlfriend in love-child riddle'.

She felt the colour drain from her face, her breathing suddenly shallow, her eyes moving avidly over the paper, the written article accompanying the headline spoke of a reliable source informing them of the illegitimate child she had given birth to several years ago. It claimed the father of the child was something she didn't talk about, that it was even a big dark secret. It also wondered what her new lover thought of this love-child. Danielle had no need to guess at the identity of the 'reliable source', but at least Audra hadn't realised that Nick had been the baby's father!

Her father crouched down in front of her. 'I'm sorry, Ellie. I have no idea how this trashy newspaper,' he threw it angrily to one side, 'got hold of such a story.'

Danielle was still too shaken to speak. She had known Audra was out for blood, but this, *this* was

too much. The other woman had found the
miniature of her beloved baby when she went
through her private things in the jewellery box,
had drawn her own conclusions about the blonde-
haired baby, and told the newspapers about it out
of spite.

'Who could have done such a thing?' her father
asked darkly. 'And why?'

She raised a shaking hand to her temple. 'That
doesn't matter now, it's done. I—Would you mind
very much if I wanted to be alone now?' she
looked at him pleadingly, willing him to understand how much she needed to be on her own just
now.

'Of course, darling,' her father held her in his
arms as she stood up. 'I have to admit, though,
that I had a feeling something like this might
happen,' he muttered grimly.

She looked up at him in stunned surprise. 'You
did?' she asked warily.

'A man like Andracas, so much in the public
eye, was bound to drag you down there with him.'

'It wasn't Nick's fault, Daddy,' she had to be
fair to him about this, he couldn't have known
Audra would do something as poisonous as this.

Her father looked down at her with concern in
his eyes. 'Then you are involved with him?'

She thought fleetingly of last night, and then
dismissed it from her mind. 'He's just an
acquaintance——'

'Ellie, you don't have to pretend with me,' he
gently interrupted. 'I didn't judge anything you
did in the past, and I'm not going to judge you
now.'

She shook her head. 'But I'm really not involved
with him.'

He arched dark brows. 'Did you see the photograph that was with the article?'

'No . . .'

He bent to pick up the newspaper, holding it out for her to look at. She gave a weary sigh at the photograph of Nick unlocking his car door outside her apartment. It showed him leaving late last night, his dark hair ruffled, a look of lazy passion still in his eyes. It was even more damning than the one of them leaving together Sunday morning.

'You are involved with him, Ellie,' her father told him softly. 'Whether you think you are or not. And the publicity could get worse, you know.'

'Worse?' she choked in a disbelieving voice. 'I don't see how it could.'

'Oh they'll speculate about the baby's father, delve into your past to try and find out who he was.'

'They won't succeed,' she said dully. 'Even he doesn't know who he is.'

Her father sighed. 'What do you think Andracas will have to say about this?'

She gave him a sharp look. 'About what?'

'The fact that you had a baby without it having a legal father. I've heard Greek men are a bit old-fashioned about things like that.'

'Not only Greek men,' her mouth twisted. 'All men think that any woman who has a baby and isn't married to the father is an easy conquest. I doubt Nick's reaction will be any different to a hundred other men's,' she dismissed contemptuously.

'You aren't lovers already?' her father seemed surprised, and knowing of Nick's reputation that wasn't so unusual.

The memory of last night flashed briefly into her

mind, and was then dismissed. Last night, as with the night seven years ago, didn't make them lovers. 'No,' she answered truthfully.

Her father seemed to visibly relax. 'Then I would advise you, unless you're actually in love with the man,' he gave her a probing glance, 'to stop seeing him.'

'I'll think about it, Daddy,' she was still too numb to think properly, to assimilate what this latest development meant in her life. 'I really will think about it,' she assured him as the worried frown reappeared between his eyes.

'All right, darling,' he gently touched her cheek. 'I'm only concerned for you, you know that.'

'Yes,' she hugged him tightly. 'And I'm grateful to you for coming and telling me about this, I would have hated to have found out any other way.'

He nodded, his arm about her waist as she walked him to the door. 'Take care, Ellie,' he kissed her warmly. 'And don't let any of them get you down.'

'I won't,' she assured him, her smile fading as soon as she had closed the door behind him.

Seven years, seven long years, and no one had even guessed she had a child. For days after it had happened she had tried to forget that night in Nick's bed, until it became obvious that fate had decreed she should have an everlasting reminder.

Her feelings had been mixed when she first discovered she was pregnant, wonder for the life she could feel growing inside her, hate for the man who had put it there. She had hated Nick then as never before, would be eternally grateful for the love and support of her parents when she had decided to keep the baby, even though she had refused to reveal the identity of the baby's father

to them. If her father had known it was Nick
Andracas he would have confronted the other man
with the knowledge, and then he would have had
the humiliating experience of being told Nick
believed her to be a whore.

Besides which, she had hated him, had wanted
nothing more to do with him. She would care for
her baby herself, would never let it be influenced
by Nicholas Andracas' cynicism and cruelty. And
she had kept to that vow.

She felt even more wary of the second ring on
her doorbell that morning. If it were the press after
more details then she didn't want to speak to
them, and if it were Nick demanding to know if it
were true she didn't want to speak to him either. It
was neither of these people, for either of those
reasons.

Audra McDonald stood on the doorstep, her
brows raised mockingly at Danielle's lack of
welcome. 'I happen to have a couple of hours free
this morning,' she walked past Danielle in a cloud
of perfume to take up a triumphant stance in the
lounge. 'And I thought I could come and sit for
you.'

Danielle had to admire the other woman's
audacity, even if the sight of her now made her feel
nauseated. 'I won't be working today,' she said
stiltedly.

'No?' auburn brows arched.

'No,' her mouth was tight.

'That's a pity,' Audra drawled, her gaze going to
the crumpled newspaper that still lay on the
coffee-table. She picked it up, her long nails vividly
scarlet against the white-grey of the paper. She
glanced over at Danielle with a self-satisfied smile.
'It's a good likeness of Nick, isn't it?' she mocked.

She shrugged. 'If you like that sort of photograph.'

'Oh I don't *like* it, far from it,' Audra threw the newspaper down again with barely concealed anger. 'But I knew as soon as I saw it that you and Nick are now lovers.'

Her mouth twisted. 'You know how he looks when he's aroused,' she remembered mockingly.

The other woman flushed. 'And how he looks when he's made love to someone,' she snapped.

Danielle's eyes flashed deeply green. 'And you gave that story to the newspapers just because you thought Nick and I had been to bed together?' she said disgustedly.

'I *know* you have,' she rasped.

'And just what did you hope to achieve by doing this to me?'

The other woman looked at her with venomous eyes. 'If I can no longer have Nick you aren't going to have him either!'

Danielle gave her a pitying glance. 'Don't you think that's a little childish?'

The other woman flushed her anger. 'If it works I don't care what it is!'

Danielle shook her head. 'You realise you won't succeed in getting Nick back this way? He'll realise, sooner or later, that you were behind this.'

'I'm hoping he does,' Audra's expression was ugly in her need for revenge. 'It's about time someone showed him that he can't control other people's lives the way he likes to.' Her eyes glittered with dislike.

Danielle could almost pity the other woman—almost. 'Did you have to involve me?' she reasoned.

'Why not?' the actress shrugged. 'I've put up

with his other women, his taking me for granted, for over a year. If you hadn't come along he might eventually have married me.'

'Why would you have wanted that if he's treated you so badly?' she frowned.

'Are you mad?' Audra derided sharply. 'If I were Mrs Nick Andracas I would never have to work again, ever. Not that I mind acting, but I don't want to do it for the rest of my life. Nick will never marry me now, but at least I have the satisfaction of knowing he'll never marry you either!'

She sighed at the other woman's vehemence. 'You only had to ask me, I could have told you I'm not interested in becoming the wife of Nick Andracas.'

'I wanted to make sure *he* wasn't interested in marrying *you*,' the other woman bit out. 'And he won't be now,' she added with relish. 'One thing that has never entered into Nick's plans are children. The domesticity of that sort of family life has never appealed to him. And fathering someone else's bastard is something he would never do,' she scorned.

Danielle was very pale, wishing she could tell the other woman exactly who the father of that bastard child had been. But the brief satisfaction she would feel over such a disclosure wouldn't be worth the furore it would cause.

'It's amazing how you've managed to keep the child a secret for so long,' Audra continued dismissively. 'What is it by the way, a boy or a girl? It's so difficult to tell when they're still babies.'

'A girl,' she said abruptly.

'She looked a pretty little thing—if you happen

to like babies. I don't,' she grimaced. 'And I don't suppose it's a baby now, that miniature must have been painted some time ago.'

'Seven years.'

'So where is your daughter now?' Audra frowned. 'Away at school or something?'

'Or something,' she nodded jerkily.

'Very wise,' the other woman drawled. 'If I ever have any children—God forbid!—I'd send them away to school too. And in your case it serves a dual purpose, the kid is out of your way, but she's also far away from being recognised as your daughter.'

'I've never been ashamed of the existence of my daughter,' Danielle told her harshly.

'Of course you haven't,' Audra mocked. 'That's why you've hidden her existence for seven years!'

'I haven't——'

'Oh don't look so stricken, Danielle,' the other woman snapped impatiently. 'I would have done the same thing in your position, especially if I were after a big fish like Nick. Well you've lost him, I'm afraid,' she said casually. 'Better luck next time. Now if you aren't in the mood to work I may as well leave.'

Both of them knew that Audra hadn't come here with the intention of posing for her portrait, that her main aim had been to gloat over Danielle's misfortune.

Danielle wondered if the other woman would feel quite so triumphant if she knew that the baby had never grown into the beautiful little girl she had promised to be at birth, that far from being sent away Danielle's daughter had given up her battle to live only ten days after she was born, her tiny body too frail to survive any longer than that.

The baby had been born prematurely, the result of Danielle falling over in the street and starting off her labour pains. Her daugher had weighed in at just over two pounds, so small she looked as if she would fit into the palm of Danielle's hand—if she had been allowed to touch her, that is. For ten days Danielle had only been able to look at her daughter through the glass of an incubator, until the night they woke her gently to tell her that the frail little baby had given up the will to live.

If she had thought she disliked Nick before it had returned with a vengeance at the death of her daughter, despising him with a bitter hatred, as if it were all his fault that her beautiful baby had died, as if the fact that he had thrown money at her mother for the time they had spent in bed together had somehow been transmitted to the baby and made her life less than worthless, as if her daughter hadn't wanted to live when she had known she had been conceived for the price of two hundred pounds!

CHAPTER SIX

WHEN Nick arrived late that afternoon she was completely composed again, had managed to rebuff the pushy attention of the two reporters that had called personally at her door for more information on the child she had once given birth to. After suffering Audra's vindictive glee earlier she felt confident enough now to deal with anyone who wanted to pry into her life.

She had expected Nick earlier than four-thirty, had thought he would be beating on her door demanding an explanation for the article they had printed about her today. When he did finally arrive he seemed very subdued, not like his usual commanding arrogance, looking at her with a glowering expression.

'Can I get you a drink?' Danielle offered lightly.

'I've already had one,' he bit out, pacing the lounge, his hands thrust into the pockets of the trousers to the grey three-piece suit he wore, the jacket unbuttoned to reveal the waistcoat taut against his flattened stomach. 'I needed it,' he added grimly.

'Then sit down,' she invited smoothly, her light green blouse and black skirt cool as well as smart. She had prepared for Nick's arrival when she changed, wouldn't meet him as the loose-moralled woman the newspapers had implied that she was.

'I'd rather stand,' he grated, stopping his pacing suddenly to look at her with narrowed eyes. 'Is it true, Danielle?' he asked abruptly. 'Do you have a child?'

She met his gaze unflinchingly. 'No,' she answered with complete honesty.

He seemed to visibly relax, closing his eyes as he sighed deeply. 'Thank God for that. I——'

'Now,' she added with soft emphasis, looking at him with cool challenge.

Nick stiffened, his eyes narrowing once again. 'What did you say?' his breathing was shallow, his face suddenly haggard as he took in what she said.

'Surely it's obvious,' she spoke with a casualness she was far from feeling, always very emotional when she talked about her daughter. 'I did have a child, a little girl, but she died, several years ago.'

'Dear God,' he groaned, one hand up to his temple in numbed disbelief. 'I didn't—I can't— Why didn't you tell me?' he rasped, angry with himself for being at a momentary loss for words.

She raised mocking brows. 'It isn't the sort of thing you blurt out over a drink one evening.'

'Damn you, you could have——'

'What?' she looked at him with coolly unflinching eyes. 'It's none of your business what happens in my life, either now or years ago. Now is it?'

'Damn you——'

'Swearing at me won't change anything,' she derided.

'Do you have any idea what it did to me to read something like that about you in that trashy newspaper?' he demanded furiously, glaring at her with accusing eyes.

'I know exactly what it was like to read something like that,' she said with cold deliberation.

'Hell, I'm sorry,' he shook his head in regret. 'I

don't know what I'm saying. It was such a shock—It would be to anyone, you have to see that.'

'Only too well,' she acknowledged flatly. 'I've had people calling me and coming here all day who were just as shocked and surprised as you are.'

His eyes narrowed once again. 'Were you married to the child's father?'

She almost choked at the irony of him asking such a thing. 'No,' she bit out.

His hands clenched into fists at his sides. 'Did you love him?'

'I thought I did, at the time,' she shrugged.

'Then why——'

'He didn't feel the same way about me,' she explained coldly. 'I was just a body to warm his bed.'

'The bastard!' Nick looked positively violent, a pulse beating erratically to his jaw.

Danielle gave him a withering glance. Didn't Nick recognise the sort of man he was to realise when he inadvertently judged himself? It would seem not. 'Do you think so?' she asked pointedly.

'Of course I—Damn it, Danielle,' he glared at her as her meaning became clear. 'There's a little bit more than that involved in our relationship.'

'Is there?'

'You know there is. God, Danielle, I wouldn't leave you by yourself in a situation like that,' he rasped angrily. 'I wouldn't leave any woman like that,' he ground out.

Danielle could have hit him right then and there, could have pummelled his chest with her fists and told him that he *had* left her like that. But she didn't do either of those things, remained outwardly calm. 'No one is accusing you of anything, Nick,' she drawled. 'But the fact that I've had a child does seem to bother you?'

'Yes! No! It was shock, that's all,' he defended impatiently at her sceptical expression.

'You do realise who told the newspapers that story about me, don't you?'

'Audra,' he confirmed harshly. 'Her contract with the play has already been terminated and her replacement found.'

Danielle felt a jolt of shock at how coldly ruthless he could be, and then chastised herself for feeling surprised by anything he did. What had happened between them last night changed nothing, his unselfishness then had just been another ploy to get her into bed with him. She could cope with her lapse better herself if she could believe that!

'She hoped to destroy my interest in you once and for all,' he continued grimly.

'And would it have done?' Danielle kept her voice even. 'If my child had been alive?'

'The situation doesn't arise, does it,' he dismissed without emotion.

'But would it?' she persisted in being given a straightforward answer, already convinced she knew what it was.

Nick looked angry at being pushed in this way. 'I want to be your lover,' he grated. 'Not become a surrogate father to some other man's mistake!'

Danielle felt a strange stillness come over her, a cold anger that made her hands shake before she put them into the pockets of her skirt out of view. If she hadn't done that she may have given in to her earlier impulse to hit him! 'Surrogate father to some other man's mistake'! How dare he, how dare he say such a thing about *their* daughter?

The final barrier had been removed from the revenge she had once planned to take on him, the secret of her daughter's birth no longer a secret, and no one, not even Nick himself, had any idea that he was the father. But that was all going to change, and very soon!

'As you've already said, the situation doesn't arise,' somehow her voice managed to sound normal.

'No,' but he still didn't sound too happy about this unexpected development in their relationship. 'Do you still see him, this man?' he looked at her with suspicion. 'The father of your child?'

'Occasionally,' she answered truthfully.

'And do you still—feel anything, for him?' Nick rasped.

'Only contempt,' she scorned.

'Then none of this changes anything between us?'

It changed everything, if he did but know it. Instead of refusing to go out with him she now intended accepting his invitations. When, and if, he made any more. And she felt sure he would. 'I didn't realise there was anything to change,' she mocked.

'You know that I want you!'

'Yes.'

'Then I don't want any more games between us,' he pulled her into his arms with savage determination. 'Will you have dinner with me tonight?'

He was so sure of himself now, so confident of her answer, that she would have loved to slap him down one more time. But her revenge was in earnest now, and she had every intention of beginning his hell as soon as possible. 'Of course,' she accepted softly. 'And what do you suggest I do with the portrait of Miss McDonald?'

'Throw it away,' he rasped. 'She certainly won't be needing it now!'

She would find much pleasure in disposing of the portrait of the woman who had deliberately set out to destroy her, but professional pride dictated she couldn't do that. 'It's almost completed, I'll send it to her.'

'Forget about Audra,' he ordered curtly. 'She's no longer important in either of our lives.'

No, the other woman had used all her leverage now, and Danielle could dismiss her as easily as Nick did. 'I'll have to change if we're going out to dinner,' she told him huskily, conscious by the rigid hardness of his body pressed against hers that he might have a change of plan in mind.

'I have to shower and change too.' He gave a rueful smile. 'I came here straight from the office when I couldn't stand the hell of imagining you the mother of another man's child any longer.'

Danielle stiffened. 'The fact that my child died doesn't alter the fact that I was her mother. I loved my daughter very much,' she rasped coldly. 'I wanted her to live more than anything else in the world.'

Nick looked as if she had physically struck him. 'You wanted the child of a man you despise?'

'She wasn't responsible for the man he was, I wanted her alive and well!'

He pushed her away from him as if he daren't touch her any more. 'I'll be back in two hours and we'll go out to dinner.' His movements were as co-ordinated as usual as he walked to the door. 'Be ready to go when I get back.'

'Nick,' the quiet control of her voice stopped him leaving. 'I won't be treated as you did Audra McDonald,' she told him with challenge. 'I'll go out to dinner with you tonight, but I won't be ordered about like one of your minions. I'll also try and be ready by the time you get back, but I'm not guaranteeing it, do I make myself clear?'

Anger gleamed in his eyes at her stubbornness. 'Only too well,' he bit out. 'I'll see you later.'

Danielle waited until he had left before relaxing the rigid control she had held over her emotions. That the subject of her child was one Nick didn't want to talk about was obvious; he preferred to just dismiss it from his mind, to even pretend it had never happened.

She had wished that too for a time after she realised she was pregnant, but as she sensed the life growing inside her, imagined the tiny baby *she* had created with her love, she had begun to want it, desperately. Her parents had been very supportive after they got over their initial shock, even more so in the weeks following the baby's death, convincing her that her life had to go on, encouraging her career as a portrait painter.

But if Nick thought her illegitimate child changed her moral beliefs he was going to be in a for a shock. She had made love with him once, and since that night there had been no one. And there would be no one else after him this time either.

She was expecting Lewis when he arrived half an hour later, had known from his call that afternoon that he would be coming round, which was why she wasn't sure if she could be ready on time for Nick. Lewis may only stay a short time, but he may stay longer.

He looked a trifle harassed as she let him in. 'I came round as soon as I could, but I seem to have been caught up in meetings all day. Are you all right?' he gave her a worried look.

'Fine,' she looked puzzled.

'I think you should sue the damned papers,' he muttered angrily. 'They shouldn't be allowed to get away with printing such lies. That rubbish they printed yesterday about you and Andracas was bad enough, but I think they went too far today.'

'Lewis——'

'I hope you've been in touch with a good lawyer,' he was very indignant on her behalf. 'They shouldn't be allowed to get away with printing slander like that.'

'Lewis, sit down,' she encouraged gently, not quite knowing how to tell him that none of what they had printed had been slanderous.

He made no effort to sit. 'If I'd realised my persuading you to take this commission when you would rather not have done would lead to such hurtful lies being printed about you I would have turned the damned thing down myself. The newspapers take a perfectly innocent incident and turn it into whatever they want to. It can't go on.'

'Lewis, it's the truth,' she said quietly.

'I don't think I've ever—— What did you say?' he asked in stunned surprise.

'Everything the newspapers said was the truth,' she repeated gently.

He seemed to swallow hard. 'Everything?' he echoed disbelievingly.

She knew she should be flattered by his surprise, but she just felt awful for disillusioning him. 'Yes,' she nodded. 'Would you like to sit down now?'

'I think I'd better,' he said dazedly, almost falling down into one of the armchairs. 'But I— I've never seen a child here, never heard you talk about one,' he said dully, looking as if she had shattered every illusion he had ever had about her.

Danielle explained the situation to him as briefly as she could, felt she had given too many people too many explanations just lately, and about things she considered very private indeed.

'But it isn't true that you've been out with Andracas, is it?' he dismissed with scorn.

'I'm afraid it is.'

Lewis frowned. 'And Audra McDonald?'

She shrugged. 'As far as I know she's no longer his mistress.'

'As far as——! But they've been together over a year!'

'Then it was probably time for a change,' she said calmly. 'For both of them.'

'Are you sure you aren't the one who will be left out in the cold? He's done this sort of thing before, you know, and he always goes back to Miss McDonald.'

'Not this time,' she told him confidently.

'But——'

'Lewis,' she cut in firmly. 'I understand the reason for your concern, and I'm grateful for it, but doesn't what I've just told you about my past convince you that I can take care of myself?'

He flushed uncomfortably at the gentle rebuke. 'I'm sorry,' he said abruptly. 'If course it's none of my business who you go out with,' he stood up. 'I had no right to try and interfere. But God, how I wish I'd never brought you this commission!'

She gave a rueful smile. 'Sometimes people are destined to meet no matter what the circumstances.'

He shook his head. 'I've never believed in fate.'

Danielle did, had known as soon as Lewis told her about the Audra McDonald portrait that it would one day come to this. It was all meant to happen, it *had* to happen!

Nick's manner had changed back again when they went out that evening, the cajoling charm and easy manner replaced by the haughty arrogance she had come to expect from him, treating her politely if not warmly. For her part Danielle treated him as she usually did, with a mixture of coolness and disdain.

The reporters were noticeably absent from trailing after them tonight, and Danielle had a feeling that was because Audra knew she had lost, that she had nothing to gain and so much more to lose. Nick could be even more ruthless than he had been, they all knew that.

She knew by the direction they were taking once they left the restaurant that he wasn't taking her home or to her apartment. For a few brief seconds she had a mad impulse to see if his apartment near the park was still the same, to see if he still had black silk sheets on the huge double bed.

But common sense took over and she dismissed the idea. 'I'd rather go home,' she told Nick coolly.

'I thought we could have a drink first——'

'We can, at *my* apartment,' she turned to look at him with unflinching eyes.

He frowned his displeasure. 'I don't intend to seduce you, Danielle.'

'I've already explained to you,' she said flatly. 'That I won't be treated like one of your mistresses.'

'It's only my apartment——'

'Where you usually entertain your "women friends",' she reminded with scorn.

'Oh all right,' he muttered, swinging the car back in the direction of her home. 'Although I can't see what the big deal is in going to my apartment.'

Danielle didn't even bother to answer him. They both knew he had intended them to do more than have a drink at his apartment, and she was determined that she wasn't going to succumb that easily. The longer she made him wait for her the more confused he was going to be when she eventually gave in.

She turned to him as he stopped the car outside her home. 'Perhaps you shouldn't come in after all,' she said in a reasoning tone. 'I'm a little tired tonight.'

'Danielle——'

'Thank you for dinner,' she leant forward and kissed him briefly on the mouth, pulling away as he would have deepened the caress. 'Perhaps we can do it again some time.'

'Danielle!' he groaned huskily, pulling her back into his arms. 'I can't let you go like this.'

She felt no sense of triumph that she had won this round, knew that she had a long way to go yet to reduce him to the humble lover she wanted him to be. 'I thought that was what you wanted,' she remained aloof in his arms. 'You've been very angry all evening.'

'Give me time,' he said raggedly. 'I'll get over it.'

She looked up at him with angry eyes. 'I'm not asking for your forgiveness, Nick. God, you wouldn't expect me to react this way if you had left a trail of illegitimate children all over the place!'

His expression became harsher than ever. 'The situation would never arise!'

'Well how clever of you,' she derided hardly. 'Unfortunately, we aren't all that lucky. I really think it would be better if we didn't see each other again.' She took a gamble on how deeply he wanted to possess her. 'I'm not about to keep justifying, or explaining myself, to you or anyone else.'

He buried his face in her throat. 'I'm not asking you to,' he said gruffly. 'And I apologise if you think I've been abrupt this evening——'

'Abrupt?' she scorned the description of his behaviour. 'You've been unbearable!'

He nodded. 'I know. And I'm sorry.' The dark grey eyes searched her face. 'God, you're beautiful,' he groaned raggedly. 'So beautiful. . . .'

She suffered his kiss rather than responded to it, the weakness that had engulfed her last night no longer there today, her anger at the way he was trying to 'forgive' her for her lapse in the past making it unnecessary to even try and resist him; she was cold in his arms.

Nick pulled away as he sensed her lack of response. 'Can I see you tomorrow?'

'Not tomorrow,' she refused.

'Why not?' he grated, obviously not pleased by her answer.

'I do have other friends I like to see besides you,' she told him coolly.

Glittering anger darkened his eyes. 'Who?'

'Really, Nick——'

'Who are you seeing tomorrow night?' his hands bit painfully into her arms.

Danielle looked at him unflinchingly, although from the pain he was inflicting she would probably have bruises there tomorrow. 'I'm visiting an old schoolfriend,' she said evenly.

'Female?'

'Of course,' she mocked.

He thrust her away from him as if she burnt him. 'Is that the truth?'

'Why should I lie?'

He heaved a ragged sigh. 'Because for some reason you seem to enjoy watching me squirm!'

Danielle pulled a face. 'The fact that I'm visiting a friend shouldn't do that to you.'

'It wouldn't,' he rasped. 'If I could be sure you were telling the truth.'

'Nick,' she spoke to him in a patient voice. 'As far as I know we don't have any chains on each other. We've been out together, officially, only once, and that certainly doesn't make a commitment to each other not to see other people if we want to.'

His eyes were narrowed to steely slits. 'You're telling me that if I chose to see Audra tomorrow that you wouldn't give a damn, is that it?'

She shrugged. 'I'd abhor your choice of companion, but I'd have no right to object.'

His face contorted with anger. 'I'm giving you that right,' he bit out harshly.

She shook her head. 'I don't want it.'

'I'm not giving it to you lightly,' he rasped. 'I just don't seem to have any choice about it. I haven't made love to any other woman since we met.'

For the second time, Danielle added mentally. He had had plenty of other women in his life in the preceding seven years. 'I thought you said my uninterest in you would make Miss McDonald suspicious and that she would be more attentive,' she mocked.

'It did,' he nodded grimly. 'I wasn't interested.'

No wonder the other woman had been so convinced, even without Danielle's encouragement of Nick, that she was losing him! 'It's a pity you didn't feel this same single-minded attraction during your marriage—for your wife,' she scorned.

Nick seemed to stiffen. 'What do you know about my marriage?' he asked tautly.

'Only that it didn't last—because of your adultery.'

'Whatever you've been told to the contrary I was never unfaithful to my wife.'

'But the newspapers——'

'Are not always given the true facts, hence they can't print them,' he grated.

'But why would you lie——'

'That is my business, Danielle,' he cut in icily. 'As you insist the birth of your child is yours.'

Danielle was puzzled by his disclosure about his marriage, she couldn't pretend that she wasn't. Although it made no difference to the way he had treated her, or to the fact that he hadn't given her welfare after that night a second thought. 'I'd better go in now——'

'Thursday night?' he halted her exit with his hand on her arm.

She pretended to give the idea some thought. 'Very well,' she finally nodded.

It was a very dangerous game she was playing, a man like Nick might crack at any moment and take what wasn't being freely given. But while she continued to treat him with that cool condescension she didn't think he would do anything like that, would be too afraid of alienating her for good. And that was something she knew he didn't want.

Rhea had changed little since they were at finishing school together, still a red-haired beauty with plenty of charm, although married life to her

television producer husband had given her an
added glow of happiness.

'Excuse the mess,' Rhea stepped over the toys
that littered most of the lounge floor. 'I've
managed to get the little horror off to sleep for the
night, now I have to put the house back together,'
she grimaced as she knelt to put the toys away in a
box. 'I never knew a two-year-old boy could have
so much energy!'

Danielle smiled at her friend, helping to pick up
the toys. 'Like mother like son . . .' she teased.

'You sound like Graham,' Rhea laughed. 'He
says he doesn't stand a chance of peace and quiet
with the two of us about.'

Danielle knew that Graham doted on his wife
and son, that he hated the evenings like this when
he had to work late as much as Rhea did. Which
was why Danielle had offered to keep her friend
company.

It didn't take them long to tidy up the lounge,
and the two of them were soon sitting down
together enjoying a relaxing cup of tea.

'So how are you?' Rhea asked lightly.

Danielle gave her an understanding smile. 'It's
all right, I'm not about to break apart at the
seams. You've seen the newspapers the last few
days?'

'Yes,' her friend nodded.

'So you know Nick is back in my life.'

'Why, Ellie?' Rhea couldn't pretend not to be
puzzled by her behaviour, the only other person to
know the whole truth about that night seven years
ago.

She looked up at her friend with a blaze of
emotion. 'Why do you think?' she choked.

'Darling, you'll get hurt——'

'But so will he be when I've finished with him,' her hands clenched into fists. 'Seven years ago I meant nothing to him, was just another body, but it's different this time, now *I* have all the power.'

'Ellie——'

'I didn't intend doing this, Rhea,' she cut across her friend's reasoning voice. 'But he expected me to meekly consent to share his bed for a few weeks. I couldn't do that and not make him pay for what happened in the past.'

'But, Ellie, he doesn't know all that happened in the past,' Rhea defended.

'He knows enough. And the rest I'll tell him.'

'But nothing you do now can change the past——'

'No,' Danielle acknowledged tautly. 'But at least I'll have the satisfaction of giving him the same humiliation he gave me. I have to do it, Rhea, so please don't try to talk me out of it.'

Her friend sighed her acceptance of the situation. 'Will you tell him about the baby being his too?'

'No,' she rasped. 'Because she was mine! I just want to give him back his money and let him see how it feels.'

Rhea looked alarmed. 'Ellie, you aren't going to——'

'I'm going to give him back his two hundred pounds for the same reason he gave it to me,' she looked at her friend unflinchingly.

'It could backfire on you——'

'It won't,' she said flatly. 'I'm immune to the "charms" of Nick Andracas.' Once again she thrust to the back of her mind the way she had reacted to him on Monday night.

And somehow she succeeded in keeping Nick at

arms' length during the following weeks, giving him that little bit more of herself when she suspected he was becoming impatient with their relationship as it was. She felt like a kitten tormenting a potentially lethal snake.

But he continued to want to see her even though she denied him a physical relationship, only occasionally showing that old ruthlessness that she disliked so much, seeming content the rest of the time to bide his time until she felt ready and willing to give him what he wanted.

The newspapers had lost interest in them a little too since the night they went to the opening night of *Broken Dolls*, Nick so affably charming to everyone that evening that there was little to write about any more. Danielle could have told them the reason for his lazy charm that night, knew that he believed her passionate response to him at her apartment before they left for the theatre meant she would later spend the night with him. The argument that had followed as a result of her refusal to do so had ended with Nick storming out of her apartment.

He had returned the next day and apologised, and since then their relationship had gone along quite smoothly. As smoothly as it ever would, or could!

'Are your mother and I ever to be introduced to him?' her father wanted to know.

The two of them were lunching together in one of London's finest restaurants, Danielle having expected to be questioned about Nick ever since she arrived ten minutes earlier; her parents had been surprisingly silent on the subject of her continuing to see Nick. 'It isn't that sort of relationship, Daddy,' she dismissed the idea lightly.

'Then what sort is it?'

She shrugged. 'Casual.'

'So casual he sees other women when he isn't with you?' her father rasped.

'If he wanted to,' she nodded, giving him a puzzled frown. Nick had insisted on seeing her almost every evening for the last few weeks; she didn't understand what had made her father ask such a question.

'And he obviously does.'

'Sorry?'

He nodded behind her. 'Andracas and one of his women,' he bit out angrily.

Danielle turned slowly so as not to draw attention to herself. Nick was just in the process of leaving the restaurant, a beautiful raven-haired woman at his side. As if sensing her gaze on him Nick turned in Danielle's direction, his whole body tensing as he looked from her to her father and then back again. The grey eyes narrowed with icy anger before he grasped the arm of the woman at his side and stormed from the restaurant.

'Arrogant bastard,' Danielle's father muttered furiously.

She turned to him with an amused smile on her lips. Whether the woman with Nick was his new mistress or not was irrelevant, his reaction to seeing her with another man, a man he obviously hadn't realised was her father, told her that he was still very attracted to her. And that was all that mattered.

'I don't like the man, Ellie,' her father added grimly, still very angry.

She gave him a teasing smile. 'Because he was having lunch with a woman?'

'Doesn't it bother you that he was?' He couldn't

seem to understand her casual acceptance of what had just occurred.

'Not particularly,' she dismissed. 'I'll still be seeing him myself, I'm sure.'

'I don't understand you, Ellie,' he shook his head, seeming dazed by her attitude.

'I'm sorry,' she touched his hand in gentle understanding, 'I really am.'

'But you'll go on seeing him anyway,' he realised dully.

She had to now, she had gone this far, she intended seeing it through to the end. But if her father thought she was just going to meekly accept seeing Nick out with another woman then he was wrong. Nick would know of her displeasure at seeing him here in the only way he seemed to understand, and that was physically.

'Yes,' she told her father softly. 'I'll go on seeing him.'

CHAPTER SEVEN

SHE was expecting the telephone call that came shortly after she got in that afternoon, had known from his furious expression earlier that Nick would contact her sooner rather than later.

'I want to see you tonight, Danielle,' he bit out without preamble.

'You know we agreed——'

'I know *you* agreed that we wouldn't meet tonight,' he ground out harshly. 'You also know the reason why it's now necessary that we see each other.'

'No——'

'I intend calling for you at eight o'clock, Danielle,' he cut in autocratically.

She could tell that he really wasn't in a mood to be pushed very far at the moment, that he was on a razor-sharp edge of telling her to go to hell. 'Very well, Nick,' she conceded coolly. 'Although I really don't see what all the urgency is about.'

'You don't see——! Who was the man lunchtime, Danielle?' he demanded angrily.

'He——'

'No, don't tell me now,' he rasped. 'I'd rather hear it when we're face to face.'

'That sounds ominous,' she said lightly.

'And isn't it?'

'Must I remind you that you were with another woman at the restaurant too?' she taunted.

'I have a perfectly good excuse for that.'

'Well so do I!'

'I'd be interested to hear it,' he rasped.

'So would I!'

'You wouldn't be jealous, would you?' he sounded pleased at the idea.

'Not in the least,' she answered instantly, her voice ringing with honesty.

'Damn you,' he swore raggedly. 'I'm calling for you at eight o'clock tonight, I would advise you to be ready when I arrive.' He rang off abruptly.

Danielle knew by his attitude that she had been right about his wrong assumption concerning her father earlier; he was going to feel very foolish when he learnt the truth. But that didn't stop her feeling curious about the woman who had been with him. Could it possibly be that he was already tiring of her unwillingness to have an affair with him and was seeking his pleasure elsewhere? If that were the case she would just have to remind him that it was *her* he wanted.

The gown she chose to wear for the evening was deliberately provocative, the black material fitting snugly to her breasts without benefit of shoulder straps, her creamy white throat completely bare. The dress showed how narrow her waist was before curving lovingly over her hips and down to the floor in gentle folds. Her hair was secured lightly on top of her head, the wispy tendrils that remained about her nape and cheeks emphasising the haunting beauty of her face.

The heavy flush of desire on Nick's face when he saw her was enough to tell her he approved of the way she looked tonight. His mouth twisted. 'Is this a way to take my mind off the fact that you were out with another man lunchtime?' he derided hardly, his stance challenging in the black evening suit as he faced her across the room.

'If it is it didn't succeed, did it?' she drawled mockingly.

His eyes narrowed at her lightness. 'Now you can tell me who he is.'

'Do you really think you have any right to demand an explanation from me?' she taunted. 'After all, you were far from alone either,' she reminded.

'That woman was my elder sister,' Nick rasped. 'She was here to ask my advice about her daughter.'

Danielle could see the family resemblance now, both to Nick and the woman's daughter, Carly. 'Do your family always run to you for help?' she derided to cover the slightly disconcerted feeling she had at hearing him talk about the mother of her old school acquaintance.

'I'm still the head of the family,' he told her arrogantly. 'I may have been born in America but we haven't completely adopted the American way of life. Even though all my sisters were married and have children we are still very much a family ourselves. But we're diverting from the point,' he suddenly realised. 'I want to know who the man was that I saw you with at lunchtime?' He looked at her coldly.

She gave him an amused smile, dismissing the fleeting idea she had had of her and Carly accidentally meeting. He hadn't said Carly was in England, only her mother. Because if she should meet the other girl she would surely recognise her, and then perhaps Nick would remember meeting her before too. 'It seems to be a day for seeing our families,' she said softly. 'The man was my father.'

Nick's eyes narrowed suspiciously, moving searchingly over her face as she looked back at him unflinchingly. 'He didn't look old enough,' he finally said slowly.

She gave a mischievous smile. 'I'll tell him you said so, it will do wonders for his ego.'

Nick still looked unconvinced that she was telling him the truth. 'Why didn't you tell me last night that you were lunching with your father today?'

'Why didn't you tell me you were lunching with your sister?' she returned smoothly.

His mouth tightened angrily. 'Because she didn't call me until this morning.'

Danielle shrugged. 'Then you have your answer to your question too, my father didn't invite me to lunch until this morning either. Really, Nick,' she snapped impatiently as he continued to glare at her suspiciously. 'You either believe me or you don't. I'm not about to get a sworn statement from my father to convince you I'm telling the truth!'

He ran a hand over his brow. 'I just wish I understood you more. We've been seeing each other for over a month now, and I'm no closer to knowing you now that I was when we first met.'

'That isn't true, Nick,' she moved close to him, her arms about his shoulders. 'I've told you quite a lot about my life. And you know all of my preferences in food and drink,' she added teasingly.

His arms moved convulsively about her waist. 'They aren't the preferences I'm interested in,' he growled.

She tilted her head to one side as she looked up at him. 'They're the only ones I care to discuss.'

'Danielle——'

'Are we going out to dinner?' she interrupted cheerfully, moving out of his arms, only intending to give him a foretaste of what he couldn't have. 'I haven't eaten yet because you didn't say earlier what your plans were for the evening.'

'That's because at the time I didn't have any plans,' he grated. 'But, yes, we're having dinner.'

Danielle knew as he drove in the direction of the park that he had lied about not having any plans for the evening, that he had intended bringing her to his apartment all along so that he could make love to her!

It was all so familiar as they went up together in the lift, although this time she actually had a chance to see what the lounge to his home was like, finding the room very comfortable with its expensive furnishings, the paintings on the walls obviously originals.

She turned to give Nick a bright smile as he watched her reaction to being brought here, his expression wary. 'Is this the part where you turn down the lights, switch on the romantic music, pick me up in your arms and carry me off to your bed?' she taunted.

He flushed his displeasure at her mockery. 'Danielle——'

'I suppose the bed has black silk sheets with which to seduce me between?' she continued to taunt, sitting down to look up at him with mocking green eyes, feeling confident of herself as she scorned him, older now, knowing the seduction for what it was and not imagining she meant any more to Nick than any other woman he could make love to.

His eyes narrowed to steely slits. 'How did you know they were black?' he rasped.

She shrugged. 'I would be disappointed in you if they weren't. Are you saying they are?' she feigned innocence.

'Yes,' he bit out.

'Really, Nick,' she chided in a mocking voice. 'I would have thought you were a little more subtle than that.'

'Subtlety hasn't worked with you so far,' he derided.

'Black silk sheets won't either,' she dismissed hardly. 'I happen to dislike them intensely.'

Nick studied her closely at the bitterness he detected in her voice. 'Your lover had black sheets on his bed,' he guessed gratingly.

'He wasn't a lover,' she said dully, the memories of this apartment overwhelming her. 'He was a professional manoeuverer, like you,' She stood up abruptly. 'I'd like to leave now.'

'No!'

'Either you take me away from here now, Nick, or I leave on my own.'

'You won't do either,' he told her grimly, coming towards her. 'I'm tired of you making all the decisions in our relationship—such as it is!—in future we'll do things *my* way.'

She could see that he meant it, that his razor-sharp mood that she had detected earlier had indeed snapped, and instead of telling her to go to hell he had decided to make love to her. 'You'll regret it if you force me,' she told him flatly.

'It won't be force, Danielle,' he pulled her roughly against him. 'At least, only at the beginning. You see, we both *know* that you respond to me.' He removed the single clip that released her hair, running his fingers through the silken tresses.

She blushed at his reminder of an evening she would rather forget, sure that this time he wouldn't get such a response, that where they were and the circumstances of Nick forcing his passion on her would make it possible for her to remain detached from his lovemaking.

But she found it increasingly difficult to remain aloof to his kisses as he caressed her lips with slow thoroughness, his tongue moving temptingly along the edge of her inner lip, delving deeper inside as she remained passive in his arms. At the same time he slid the zip at the back of her gown down to her waist, the material falling away from her pert breasts without this support.

His hand was warm against her breast as it cupped beneath it, holding the nipple up to his questing lips. Danielle felt the familiar weakness engulf her, fighting the pleasure that coursed through her body, determined not to give Nick the satisfaction of knowing how weak she was when he touched her like this.

But he was far from finished with her, his thumbtip moving across the nipple in erotic rhythm as his mouth returned to hers, parting her lips wide, encouraging her to deepen the kiss to the intimacy he desired. Like an automaton she did so, instantly feeling the rush of desire that pulsed through his body, his groan low in his throat. Now he was once again the aggressor, bending her back over his arm to kiss a trail of fire across her throat and down to the tempting swell of her breasts, moving even lower as he fell to his knees in front of her.

'No!' she groaned her anguish. 'Not that. Please!' she begged him to stop.

He leisurely explored her navel before standing up. 'I want to know every inch of you, Danielle,' he told her deeply. 'To kiss every part of you.'

She wanted it too, wanted the slow ecstatic lovemaking she knew he could give her!

She had no memory of being picked up in his arms, intoxicated by the sweet sensuality of his sweat-dampened skin, only coming to her senses as she felt the softness of silk sheets beneath her naked back.

'No!' She got up off the bed as if it burnt her, staring in horrified fascination at the black sheets, suddenly aware of how close she had come to being seduced beneath those sheets for a second time.

Nick looked puzzled by her reaction. 'Danielle, they're only sheets——'

'*Black silk* ones,' she said with distaste, pulling her gown up to re-zip it.

'All right,' he flushed his anger. 'I'll take the damned things off the bed.' He began to pull at them.

She shook her head. 'It's too late for that.'

His eyes glittered with fury as he glared across the bed at her, his dark hair ruffled to disorder, his shirt unbuttoned almost to his waist to reveal the curling dark hair against his chest. 'You're the most complicated woman I know,' he snapped.

'I'm sorry.'

'Like hell you are! God, I don't know a thing about you. You won't let me near you!'

She looked down contemptuously at the rumpled bed. 'Not like that I won't.' She turned and left the room, knowing he followed her back into the lounge.

'I can't reach you any other way!' he rasped. 'Even you can't control that response for long.'

'Even me?' she echoed softly, looking at him coldly.

'You're like ice the rest of the time,' he told her grimly. 'Do you ever intend to let me make love to you?' His eyes were narrowed.

'It isn't a question of allowing it——'

'Do you?' he persisted darkly.

She shrugged. 'Perhaps not.'

A pulse jerked in his jaw. 'Then why the hell are you going out with me?'

Danielle looked at him with emotionless eyes. 'All right,' she said softly. 'I won't see you again.'

Nick watched in dazed disbelief as she picked up her clutch-bag and quietly left. But he made no attempt to stop her.

She was shaking badly by the time she reached the pavement and hailed a taxi. This time she really may have pushed him too far! If she had then the torture of the past few weeks had all been for nothing.

The next week brought no word from Nick, although the gossips reported that he had a new woman in his life, a sweet young actress whom Danielle felt would be utterly cowed by him in a matter of days rather than weeks. The news of his new mistress was a great disappointment to her, and halfway through the second week after she had walked out on him she decided to take the holiday she had been promising herself for months, flying out to Florida to laze in the sun for a couple of weeks and think out her future, decide what she was going to do about Nick. As she saw it she had only two alternatives, she either left things as they were between them or she did the equivalent of crawling back to him. Neither was acceptable to her.

She was in no hurry to return to London, lingering another week on the palm-edged beaches,

her eyes opening wide as she came back from a swim
in the clear blue water one afternoon to find Lewis
stretched out on a beach towel next to hers, his body
very white in the blue swimming trunks against the
tan she had acquired the last two and a half weeks.

'Is there anything wrong?' She picked up a towel
to dry her hair, her black bikini slicked to the
slender curves of her body.

He moved up to lean back on his elbows. 'Not
from where I'm lying,' he grinned.

'Lewis——'

'Nothing is wrong,' he cried defensively. 'You
seemed very vague about when you were coming
back when you telephoned me the other day, so
I've come out here to make sure you go back in
the next couple of days.' He looked up appreciatively at the clear blue sky. 'Although I
might stretch it into a week,' he added lazily. 'It
was raining when I left England.'

Danielle sat down cross-legged next to him on
her towel. 'What's the rush?' she frowned.

'I have a couple of commissions lined up for
you,' he shrugged.

'Is that all it is?' she asked with a casualness she
was far from feeling.

He gave her a sideways glance. 'What else could
there be?'

She turned away to hide her disappointment.
'Nothing. Did you happen to see my parents
before they left?'

He nodded. 'They sent their love.'

She bit her lip, choosing her next words
carefully. 'Have you seen anything of Nick lately?'

'Nick?'

'Andracas,' she enlarged tightly, having the
distinct impression Lewis was playing with her.

'Oh that Nick,' he nodded again. 'Yes, I've seen him, a couple of times, in fact.'

'And?'

'He seemed fine,' Lewis shrugged.

'Oh.'

'Physically, that is,' he added ruefully. 'His temper could do with a bit of improving, though. Do you know, he threatened to punch me on the nose unless I told him where you were?' He feigned surprise.

Danielle felt a surge of hope, her earlier disappointment forgotten. 'He did?'

'Yes. Strange that,' Lewis mocked. 'Of course I didn't tell him.'

'Oh,' her disappointment returned, although she looked at him suspiciously as he continued to look unperturbed. 'You don't exactly have the look of someone who has recently been hit.' His handsome face looked as clean-cut as it usually did.

'Of course not,' he smiled. 'I'm not stupid. I told him I couldn't possibly break a confidence, but that I would let you know he wanted to see you.'

'What did he say to that?'

Lewis grimaced. 'I wouldn't offend the delicacy of a lady by repeating his answer,' he said dryly. 'But he did warn me that if anyone, including you, were to learn through me that he had been looking for you that I could be in serious trouble. I have no idea what he could have meant, do you?' he mocked.

Danielle couldn't help but smile. 'You're taking this very well, I know that.'

'What else can I do?' he shrugged. 'My priority must lie with you. After all,' he grimaced. 'Andracas can only beat me to a pulp, you pay my wages.'

She laughed softly. 'My hero!'

'Seriously, Danielle,' he sobered suddenly. 'What's going on between you two?'

'Not a lot at the moment,' she told him truthfully, although it sounded as if Nick had had a change of heart about that.

'The last I heard he was going out with Jemima Street. Then suddenly that was all over, and——'

'It is?' she queried sharply.

Lewis nodded. 'He found her a part in one of the plays he's promoting as her pay-off. Not bad for spending a few weeks in his bed.'

'You're becoming cynical, Lewis,' she derided.

'I know,' he sighed. 'That's what happens when you have your life threatened by one of the most powerful men in the world! So what is going on?'

She shrugged. 'I think I shall have to go back to London to find that out.' Although her hopes had been raised tremendously the last few minutes. If Nick were looking for her it could only be for one reason. 'But I think we'll stay on here a few more days,' she told Lewis firmly. 'Your tan could do with improving.'

He raised blond brows. 'What tan?'

'Exactly,' she laughed, handing him her sun-tan lotion.

In the end they stayed on a further three days, Lewis finally deciding he valued his life as well as his pay-cheque. But one thing Danielle could have done without was the reporters at the airport, ignoring their probing questions as she and Lewis climbed into a taxi.

When she saw the picture of them together in the evening newspaper later that day she wished they had answered the questions, then perhaps they wouldn't have had to invent their story!

'Danielle Smith and friend arriving from Miami', the caption read. The two of them looked tanned and fit, if a little tired after their flight, Danielle's hair bleached almost white in places from the strong sun.

She spent the evening with her parents, telling them all about her holiday and catching up on all their news. All of them avoided mentioning Nick, although her parents must have been aware of the fact that the two of them were no longer seeing each other.

She recognised the silver Ferrari parked outside her home as she parked her car just after ten, needing an early night after her long day. Nick's unexpected presence here didn't seem to indicate that she was going to get one.

He got out of his car as soon as he saw her, walking towards the building, swinging her round to face him. 'Is he the father?' he demanded fiercely.

The last month had changed Nick considerably, his face harsher than ever, his body looking leaner, despite what Lewis said to the contrary. She knew Nick's body intimately, and he had lost weight the last four weeks.

But his accusations hadn't changed, and she bristled angrily. 'If you're talking about Lewis, then the answer is no,' she snapped. 'You might be surprised by the answer.'

'Tell me.'

Temper flared in her flashing green eyes. 'Your arrogance is no less acceptable to me now than it was before,' she shook off his hand. 'I don't have to tell you *anything*.'

Once again he made no effort to stop her as she walked away, and this time Danielle had a feeling he wouldn't show any sign of weakening towards her.

She didn't know what to do. Nick was a proud man, it had taken a lot for him to come to her tonight, even if his main emotion had been anger. She doubted he would be back. Which left it up to her to be the one to make the first move. It was something she didn't like doing any more than he did.

She tried telephoning his apartment, and when she received no answer there she tried the house. A woman answered when the call was put through to the lounge.

'Who's calling?' the woman wanted to know when Danielle asked for Nick.

'I—Just a friend,' she evaded answering directly. 'But if he's busy——'

'Oh he isn't busy,' the woman derided. 'Just a moment, please.'

'Yes?' Nick rasped when he finally came on the line, his voice slightly slurred, giving Danielle the impression that when the woman had said he 'wasn't busy' in that tone she had really meant he was slightly drunk!

'It's Danielle,' she told him quickly. 'But I seem to have caught you at a bad moment——'

'Don't hang up,' he ordered harshly. 'It's only my niece. Carly, get the hell out of here,' he seemed to turn away from the receiver. 'This call is private.'

Carly! Danielle almost dropped the receiver in her shock. She had been speaking to *Carly Daniels*, Nick's niece that she had been to finishing school with, not some woman he had picked up to spend the rest of the night with as she had at first assumed. But she hadn't recognised the other woman's voice, so there was little chance of Carly recognising hers. Nevertheless, it made things difficult to know that the other woman was in London.

'Danielle, are you still there?' his voice had softened, obviously alone now.

'Yes.'

'God, you don't know how good it is to hear your voice,' he said huskily, all traces of the slur gone now. 'What happened earlier, I was out of line.'

'And I should have been more reasonable,' she sighed, relieved it was going so well between them. 'But you should know by now how the newspapers distort things.'

'You have been in Florida with Vaughn, I checked.'

She bit back her indignation that he should dare to probe into her private affairs like that. 'Then you must also know that we stayed in separate hotels,' her voice was taut. 'I'm sure you and Miss Street didn't even stay in separate *rooms*,' she added sharply.

'Danielle——'

'I didn't call you to argue with you again, Nick,' she cut in firmly. 'I wanted to invite you over to dinner tomorrow evening. I thought we could talk, calmly,' she added pointedly.

'I'd love to. . . .'

'But,' she finished dryly. 'If it isn't convenient for you then let's take a rain-check on the idea. You call me and let me know when you're free,' her voice was brittle, wondering if she were too late, if he had found a replacement for Jemima Street already. She hadn't thought of that.

'It isn't that at all—Hell, what time tomorrow?' he bit out impatiently.

'About seven-thirty?'

'I'll be there,' he told her grimly.

As it turned out they didn't speak much at all before or during the meal, Nick more reserved than she had ever seen him, the epitome of the polite dinner guest, even bringing the wine and a red rose for the centre of the table. Danielle eyed him warily; it was almost like waiting for the ice to break beneath you. Because she knew it would sooner or later.

'Lewis mentioned when we were on holiday that you wanted to see me,' she opened the conversation once they returned to the lounge with their brandies, hoping Lewis would forgive her for disclosing this confidence.

Nick's eyes narrowed. 'I simply wondered where you had disappeared to, that was all.'

That wasn't all, and they both knew it. 'I just took my holiday that was cancelled when I did Miss McDonald's portrait. I'm surprised you noticed my absence with Miss Street to keep you company,' she added mockingly.

'You know damn well I was only seeing her because you wouldn't go out with me,' he rasped.

'It wasn't a question of not going out with you, you were demanding more than I wanted to give.'

They both fell silent after her outburst, Danielle stubbornly so, Nick seeming to be searching for the right words to say.

'Nick——'

'Danielle——'

Finally they both spoke at once. 'You first,' she invited with an embarrassed laugh, uncertain and off-balance with this new Nick. His arrogance she could handle, even his blazing anger, but she couldn't even understand this different Nick, let alone handle him. It wasn't the first time he had put her off-guard with his change of manner, and she was beginning to realise there was a lot more to Nick Andracas than the lazy charm or cynical cruelty.

He sighed. 'I was just going to say that I wasn't just out of line last night, that I've been out of line all through our relationship, I realise that now.'

Danielle stiffened warily, wondering if she had misjudged his reason for coming here tonight; it sounded distinctly as if she were going to get the Andracas brush-off. 'Oh?' she sounded only mildly interested.

'Yes.' He stared into the bottom of his brandy glass. 'I've been trying to push you into an affair you've made it obvious you don't want or need. You're right, we don't even know each other, have no basis to go jumping into bed together. But when I get back from the States——'

'You're going away?' she queried sharply.

He nodded. 'That was the reason seeing you tonight was a little inconvenient. I had reservations for my niece and myself on a flight for this morning.'

'And you cancelled those plans because of me,' she realised dazedly.

His eyes were compelling. 'It was important that I see you before I go, try to make amends between us. I have to go back to the States tomorrow, I have no choice, my niece Carly is having a battle at the moment with the rest of the family about the man she wants to marry. I've been dragged in to decide if he's a suitable husband for her or not. As if I'm any judge on marriage,' he added abruptly. 'But when the family needs me, I have to go. You understand that?'

'Yes.' She could also understand Carly's insistence that she be allowed to marry the man she wanted to; the other woman had shown in the past that she had a determination and will as strong as that of her uncle.

Nick stood up, putting down his glass to come and sit on the arm of her chair. 'Your way of doing things is new to me,' he told her throatily. 'I'm not used to waiting any length of time for what I want, but with you I'm going to try.' One of his hands moved to cup her cheek. 'When I get back from America we'll do things your way for a change.'

Danielle moistened her lips, the gentleness of his caressing hand doing strange and wonderful things to her equilibriu. 'How long will you be away?'

'A week, possibly two. But I'll call you every day if I can.' His gaze was warm on her parted lips.

Possibly as long as two weeks! God, she wouldn't wait as long as that to put an end to this, things were starting to go wrong again already. She reached up to curve her arm about his neck. 'We don't have to wait that long, do we?' she encouraged huskily.

'Danielle . . .!' he groaned his confusion with her change in behaviour before lowering his head down to hers. 'It's been so long since I held you, darling,' he moaned. 'So long!'

His body crushed down on hers above her in the chair, his kiss all enveloping, his thighs moving restlessly against her. But he made no attempt to touch her intimately, even though the thin blue gown only had two tiny buttons holding the bodice up above her breasts.

Danielle moved against him impatiently, en-

couraging him to intimacy, one slender hand
moving to caress the hardness of his thighs, feeling
him shudder in reaction. Suddenly he was putting
her away from him, standing up to move away
from her, his eyes almost black from the effort it
cost him to turn away from her.

'Nick, why——'

'If I make love to you now,' his voice was gruff
with desire, 'then I'll never get to New York. And
I have to go. But when I get back I have such
plans for us!'

'Yes,' she agreed dully.

'Unless you would like to come with me
tomorrow?' he suggested with eagerness. 'I'd enjoy
showing you New York.'

'No,' she refused abruptly. 'I—I can't. I have
commitments here, my own work to do.'

'Oh,' he grimaced his disappointment. 'But
you'll save the weekend I come back for me?'

'Yes,' she said curtly. 'You really can't stay
tonight?' and looked up at him pleadingly, one
night being all she wanted.

He shook his head regretfully. 'I really have to
go tomorrow. But we'll have all the time we want
once I get back,' he promised softly.

When he got back. She both looked forward to
and dreaded that time. And it was for all the
wrong reasons!

God, she had planned this all so carefully, she
would let Nick make love to her, leave him his two
hundred pounds and then get out of his life. Only
it wasn't working out that way. She had *wanted*
him to make love to her just now, hadn't given a
damn about thoughts of revenge. She had just
wanted Nick.

And that could be very dangerous.

CHAPTER EIGHT

NICK kept to his promise and telephoned her every day, his conversation light and chatty, telling her with regret that he had to stay on a few extra days to attend his niece's wedding. Obviously he had approved of the prospective bridegroom. Which was probably as well, remembering Carly from the past she would have married the man of her choice anyway.

'I'll be back on Sunday,' Nick continued huskily.

'That's good,' she kept her own voice light, as she had done the last two weeks.

'Good!' he groaned at the inadequacy of the description, impatient with the distance that separated them. 'I want you so badly that Carly's fiancé could look like Frankenstein and I'd still approve of him just to get this problem off my hands so that I can come back to you. The last couple of weeks over here without you have been hell, Danielle.'

For her too, but for a different reason. She was fighting herself as well as him now, knew that she was no longer impersonal in her revenge, that she wanted him as badly as he claimed to want her. And that terrified the life out of her. What if she couldn't say goodbye after that one night with him? What if she fell into her own trap? She had a sad feeling she may already have done that.

'Sunday isn't too far away,' she dismissed lightly, confident of her ability to resist him with thousands of miles separating them.

'To me it is,' he grated, the cool politeness he had shown her during his other calls the last two weeks rapidly disappearing. 'Will you stay with me on Sunday night?'

She felt a leap of her pulses. 'At your apartment?'

'No,' he told her quickly. 'At my house.'

'Your house?' she repeated in a puzzled voice, sure he had never stayed overnight there with any of his women before. 'Perhaps you prefer my apartment?' She kept her fingers crossed that he would say no to the latter; she could hardly walk out of her own apartment at the end of the evening!

'No, not your apartment,' he said instantly. 'The house will be fine. I should be back by mid-afternoon, so I'll call for you at about——'

'No, I'll make my own way there,' she told him abruptly. 'I'm sure you'll be tired.'

'Not that tired,' he growled.

'Nevertheless, I'll drive myself over,' she insisted huskily.

'If that's what you want,' he accepted her independence, although his reluctance to do so indicated he didn't like it. 'You'll come over as soon as you can?'

'As soon as I can,' she echoed, a plan forming in her mind as she repeated the words.

He rang off with his usual reluctance, leaving Danielle to her thoughts. 'As soon as she could', meant exactly that as far as she was concerned. Nick wasn't the victor yet, although he may think he was. She had one more ploy to play. And he was going to be furious about it. Maybe that anger was what she needed to help her through Sunday night—his gentleness utterly defeated her.

She left her apartment early on Sunday morning, not willing to take any chances of Nick getting back earlier than he had said and coming over to surprise her. The countryside was beautiful this time of year, and after parking the car she took a small packed lunch out of the back to walk for miles across Windsor Park, choosing a private spot for her picnic, needing to be completely alone while she contemplated the folly of her actions. Nick wasn't just going to be angry about this, he was going to be furious. And she knew from experience that when he was that angry he hurt her. It would be far from the first time!

Driving back to town later that afternoon she saw a film advertised that she had been wanting to see for some time, parking her car behind the cinema to join the queue going inside. It was a good film, and at any other time she would have enjoyed it. But not when her stomach was churning at the consequences of what she was doing. She may just have gone too far this time, although it was too late to back down now, it was already almost ten o'clock now, and by the time she got home it was going to be after eleven.

Maybe she wasn't concentrating on her driving as well as she should have been, or maybe the other driver really had been at fault as the man later apologetically claimed that he had. By that time she had arrived at the hospital in the ambulance, the cuts on the arm she had received when she instinctively protected her face from the shattered windscreen serious enough to receive stitches and an overnight observation in a hospital bed. The latter she had protested as unnecessary, but the young doctor on duty had insisted that she do so.

The throbbing pain from the numerous cuts in her arm when she woke up the next morning told her that he had probably been right to insist, she even needed help to eat the breakfast they brought her. But she made sure they discharged her immediately after she had eaten, knowing she was going to have some explaining to do when she got home; Nick wasn't going to take her sudden disappearance calmly.

As she had known there would be there were half a dozen messages from him on her answering service, the first two concerned, the second two mildly angry, the last two explosive, demanding to know where the hell she was.

Her plans for last night had gone sadly awry, and with a resigned shrug she got a taxi over to the Andracas house. In normal circumstances she would have apologised to him for worrying him. Although the latter calls hadn't sounded worried, just angry.

She was shown into the lounge while she waited for Nick, formulating in her mind what she was going to say to him. When he burst into the room a few seconds later she didn't have time to say anything, Nick was saying it all!

'If last night was your idea of another game then you're the only one playing,' he began angrily. 'Just where were you all night?' he demanded to know.

'Nick——'

'I waited up for you until two o'clock in the morning. *Where were you?*' he moved forward to grasp her arms, his eyes narrowing as she gasped and noticeably paled. 'What is it?' he asked sharply. 'What's wrong?'

'My arm,' she managed to choke through the

pain he was inflicting. 'Please, let go of it!'

He removed his hands as if he burnt her, seeming to notice for the first time that she held her right arm awkwardly, gently pushing back the sleeve of her jacket to reveal the start of the bandage she wore. 'What happened?' he looked at her closely, his anger starting to fade. 'Danielle, what have you done?'

'I had a slight disagreement with the windscreen of my car,' she told him lightly.

An emotion akin to pain flickered across his arrogant face. 'Where did you spend last night?' he was no longer demanding, just enquiring.

'In hospital. Another car crashed into me.'

'God,' he groaned, closing his eyes for a moment. 'Were you badly hurt?'

She shook her head, aware that he still supported her arm with gentle hands. 'Just my arm. It seems it's instinctive to try and protect your face when something like that happens. My arm is quite badly cut in places.'

'Thank God it *wasn't* your face, then!' he ground out.

Her mouth twisted. 'Yes. I don't suppose you would find me in the least attractive if it had been.'

He folded her gently against him, careful not to touch her arm in any way. 'I'd desire you even if I couldn't see you,' he told her huskily. 'Just the feel and scent of you drives me to distraction.' He moved back slightly so that he could look down at her. 'You're sure you weren't injured anywhere else?'

'I'm sure.'

He frowned. 'Shouldn't you have your arm in a sling or something to support it?'

Danielle grimaced. 'Have you ever tried to dress trussed up in one of those things? It's impossible!'

'But you should be wearing one?' he persisted with his usual determination.

'I left it at home. I couldn't get my jacket on with it in the way.'

Barnham can pick that up with the rest of your things,' Nick decided arrogantly.

Her eyes were wide with alarm. 'What rest of my things? And who is Barnham?'

'Barnham is my butler. And you obviously can't stay at your apartment on your own with your arm out of action; you're going to come and stay here until your arm is better.'

'Nick——'

'Shame on you, Danielle,' he mocked her warning tone. 'I've never yet had to resort to making love to an injured woman. I just want you where I can make sure you're being well looked after,' he added seriously.

'My parents can take care of me——'

'No,' he told her autocratically. 'I want you *here*.'

Her brows rose. 'And are you in the habit of getting what you want?'

'Always,' he replied without hesitation.

She had to smile at his unhidden arrogance. 'I'm not sure it's what *I* want.'

'I didn't ask, Danielle, I told.' His eyes darkened to stormy grey. 'Do you have any idea what I went through last night?' he groaned. 'I don't think I slept at all, wondering what had happened to you. I came back from New York with such plans for us, and when you didn't turn up . . .!'

'You were disappointed,' she mocked.

'I was furious,' he ground out. 'Before I went

away you were so different, more affectionate than I've ever known you to be. But I sensed you were drawing away from me while I was away, and you didn't seem to be as eager for last night as I was. When you didn't arrive in time for the dinner I'd asked to be especially prepared I thought you had changed your mind and decided you didn't want to see me after all. But the answerphone at your apartment seemed to imply you were out somewhere, so I hoped you were on your way here. So I kept waiting, and hoping, and the longer I waited the madder I got. It never even occurred to me that you could have been involved in an accident.'

'I was on my way here——'

'Then it was *my* fault——'

'Don't be ridiculous, Nick,' she frowned at how pale he suddenly seemed. 'The man drove into me, not the other way around.'

'But even so——'

'I don't want to argue about whose fault the accident was,' she told him, suddenly weary. 'Would you mind if I just sat down for a few minutes?'

'Of course not,' he was instantly contrite. 'Hell, I'm sorry, Danielle. I've been so on edge the last two weeks, that I—Is it going to hurt you if I kiss you?' he groaned hungrily.

She gave a wan smile as she sank down on to the sofa. 'Not as long as you don't get too rough.'

'I'll be as gentle as a lamb,' he promised, taking her in his arms to softly caress her mouth with his lips and tongue.

The last two weeks hadn't dulled her desire for him at all, her lips parting beneath his, her body arching against him as he caressed the slenderness of her back.

His eyes were black with desire when he finally pulled away from her. 'I think I'd better go and ask Margaret to prepare a room for you,' he told her ruefully. 'Before I try and do something that's virtually an impossibility at the moment.'

Danielle expression revealed her own disappointment. 'Is it so impossible? I could——'

'We'll wait until you're completely well,' he stood up, away from the temptation of her inviting body. 'The first time between us is going to be perfect, in every way.'

The 'first time' between them *had* been perfect, in a lot of ways. Nick had made love to her with an expertise that couldn't fail to bring about a response in her, it had only been afterwards, when he insulted her with every word he spoke that she had grown to hate him.

'If that's what you want,' she nodded woodenly. 'Although I think now that I'll have to lie down for a while,' she was very pale. 'I feel a little tired.'

'Of course you do,' he realised self-disgustedly. 'I've been thoughtless. I'll go and see about your room now.' He touched her lips with his fingertips before he left the room, as if he felt a compulsive urge to keep touching her.

Margaret turned out to be the housekeeper, in fact the household seemed to be run by a whole army of servants, all of them devoted to granting Nick's slightest whim. Whatever he had told the housekeeper about her the other woman treated her as if she were an honoured guest, the bedroom she was shown into lavish enough for royalty to sleep in, the gold and lemon decor adding to its richness.

'Mr Andracas wants you to get straight into bed,' the middle-aged woman told her cheerfully, pulling the curtains. 'You're to have a nice rest and then I'll bring you up a nice lunch.'

'Oh but——'

'Mr Andracas hoped you wouldn't mind wearing this until your own things arrive,' she laid out a turquoise silk nightgown on the bed. 'It belongs to Mrs Daniels,' she added by way of an explanation for its presence here in an essentially male household.

'There's really no need for all this trouble on my account,' Danielle told the other woman. 'I can just sit in the chair and rest until my things arrive.'

'Mr Andracas' instructions were that you were to get in the bed.'

And by the look of the other woman she intended seeing that he was obeyed! 'Very well,' Danielle accepted gracefully. 'But could you tell Nick—Mr Andracas, that I would like to speak to him before he sends anyone for my clothes?'

She was snugly tucked up in bed, her arm in a makeshift sling, by the time Nick came into the room a few minutes later, although she felt very self-conscious in the sheer nightgown.

Nick's eyes were a warm velvety grey as he came to sit on the side of the bed. 'I couldn't send anyone for your things until I had the key, anyway,' he teased her.

A soft blush coloured her cheeks. 'I never thought of that.'

'I've called your parents, by the way, and told them where you're staying.'

'Oh,' it was said sharply, her eyes narrowed questioningly.

'Mm,' he nodded. 'Your father said he would call over later today to see if you needed anything. I think he just wants to check that I'm not keeping you here against your will,' Nick derided. 'Now, what was it you wanted me to bring back from your apartment for you?'

'You?' she echoed brittly.'But I thought you said you were sending Barnham.'

He smiled. 'I decided I didn't like the idea of another man touching your intimate clothing.'

'But shouldn't you be at work?' She didn't relish the thought of him going through her 'intimate clothing' either!

'I'll go in later,' he mocked. 'I do have a pretty good idea of what a woman needs for a few days' stay, you know,' he added teasingly.

'I'm well aware of that,' she said waspishly, and then cursed herself for showing that much emotion about his intimate knowledge of women. Her eyes were hard as she looked at him. 'What I wanted to ask was that you bring the green onyx jewellery box from my dressing-table too.'

His mouth quirked, a look of triumph in his eyes for what he believed to have been her show of jealousy. 'What's in there, the family secrets?'

Dark anger flashed in her eyes, making them shine like emeralds. 'What I have in there is none of your business!' She flung back the bedclothes and stood up. 'I don't think this is a good idea after all,' she told him woodenly. 'I'd rather stay with my parents.'

Nick stood up slowly, puzzlement in his expression. 'I was only teasing you just now——'

'I don't care what you were doing,' her nerves were completely strung out now. 'I want to go home.'

'I can't let you do that,' he told her softly. 'Now go back to bed like a good girl.'

'Girl?' she flinched away from him. 'I'm not a

girl!' She was breathing hard in her agitation, the dusky aureole of her breast clearly visible through the thin material of the nightgown.

There was a dark flush to Nick's cheeks as he looked at her, his eyes languorous with longing. 'I know exactly what you are, Danielle,' he said raggedly. 'And if you think this added denial is any easier on me than it is on you then you're mistaken.'

He had mistaken her taut nerves to be sexual tension—and she intended to let him go on thinking that! 'I'm sorry, Nick,' her expression lightened. 'But would you mind bringing me the jewellery box?'

'Of course not,' he bent to kiss her lightly, moving away with firm determination as his body began to stir with desire.

He did indeed seem to know what a woman needed for a few days' stay, even remembering to bring her make-up bag when he returned an hour later. As soon as she was alone Danielle checked the contents of the jewellery box, wondering if Nick's curiosity had got the better of him. Not that he would have learnt much from the money and the miniature, her baby daughter looking nothing like him. But nothing had been disturbed.

Her parents were very concerned about the accident when they arrived later that afternoon, although accepting her relationship with Nick for what it was supposed to be they didn't question the fact that she was a guest in his house.

Nick proved to be very attentive the next few days, his company never demanding as he set out to amuse her, ensuring that her slightest wish was granted.

Her arm almost completely healed, she was ready to go home. And after staying with Nick like this, coming to know the gentler side of him, she knew she couldn't see him again once she left here; she was becoming too involved with him. And he with her!

'Mm, I could quite get used to this,' Nick relaxed back in his chair one night after dinner about a week after insisting she stay with him.

Danielle looked at him sharply, understanding his meaning immediately. 'I thought domesticity wasn't your scene,' she taunted.

He shrugged. 'I don't think I've ever really encountered it until just recently. Beverley was more interested in going out and having a good time than staying at home just the two of us. Enforced celibacy has its compensations. Without all that heated passion to cloud the issue you can actually get to know the person you're interested in.'

Her hands tightened on the brandy glass she held. 'Is that a good thing?'

His eyes narrowed. 'Of course.'

She carefully placed her glass down on the coffee table. 'The police came to see me today while you were at work.'

Nick frowned. 'About the accident?'

'Yes,' she nodded. 'They just wanted to assure me that all the tests they did on the other driver were negative.'

'What tests?' he was suddenly very tense.

Danielle moistened her lips, having deliberately introduced a subject that would ultimately antagonise Nick. It was time to end this, and she wanted Nick angry when she did. 'To see if he was drunk, of course,' she dismissed coolly.

'Why would they suppose he had been drinking that time of night?' he sounded puzzled.

She mentally prepared herself for the explosion to come. 'Well it was almost eleven o'clock——'

'What?'

She looked at him calmly. 'The accident happened shortly before eleven.'

Nick sprang to his feet, glancing at her often as he tried to take in this information. 'But I thought—I thought you said you were on your way to see me?' he demanded.

'I was,' she nodded.

'At *eleven o'clock*?'

She shrugged. 'You said as soon as I could make it, and that was the earliest I could get away.'

'Eleven o'clock?' His eyes glittered with his rising anger. 'You were supposed to spend the evening with me!'

'As I remember it you only mentioned the night,' she reminded him coolly.

'Yes, but I meant—You knew damned well what I meant! Before I went away we discussed your spending the weekend with me,' he said accusingly.

'That was before you went away,' she dismissed.

'Are you telling me,' he spoke softly, slowly, 'that you intended turning up here at eleven o'clock at night for the sole purpose of spending the night with me?'

'It was all we both wanted, wasn't it?' she pointed out calmly.

'It wasn't all I wanted!'

'Then I must have misunderstood you,' she looked at him with cold green eyes.

'You didn't misunderstand me, Danielle,' he

grated. 'You knew exactly what you were doing. Is that really all you want from me, to go to bed with me?'

'Yes,' she bit out tautly.

'Then you're going to get your wish!' He strode across the room to pull her to her feet, dragging her behind him towards the stairs. 'Let's hope it's worth it,' he ground out viciously as he pushed her into his bedroom.

It was an utterly masculine room, entirely suited to the arrogant man at her side. For a moment she felt panic, reluctance to go through with this, and then she looked at Nick. He was once again the disdainful cynic she had first met, the man who had taken her so callously and then dismissed her as cruelly when his needs had been satisfied. Only this time he would have no need to accuse her of being 'mechanical' in her response—she would give him a response like he had never known before!

'Yes, let's hope it is,' she murmured as she began to take off her clothes, seeing his eyes widen in surprise at her action. 'We can hardly make love with our clothes on,' she taunted him.

'No,' he rasped, angrily pulling off his tie before he too began to undress.

His body was just as magnificent as she remembered, and as she kissed and caressed him she knew this was what had been denied her the last time they made love, that he had been intent then only on subjugating her, of making her body dance to his commands. But he couldn't stop her now, or his own reaction as she touched him intimately, his body leaping with desire.

'Danielle . . .!' his cry was partway between a groan of hunger and a plea for her to stop.

But she didn't do the latter, refused to give him

any respite to the aching satisfaction she wanted him to feel. Finally he could stand her caresses no longer, rolling her over on to her back, possessing her with a savage thrust of his body, as if he wanted to punish her for giving him so much pleasure.

Danielle hadn't wanted to feel any of that pleasure herself, but the heated warmth began to invade her body with each new thrust of his thighs, and when Nick's passion exploded into ecstasy she knew she had reached the summit with him, her whole body pulsating with a sensitivity that made her tremble.

Nick gave her a long speaking glance as he moved to lie at her side, a dark flush to his cheeks as the sleep of the satiated overcame him. Danielle lay looking down at him for several minutes, too weak herself to move very much, knowing that the two of them had reached a moment of ecstasy shared by few, that Nick had been as moved by the moment as she was.

With one last lingering look she left his bed to quietly dress, going back to her own bedroom to pack her things. When Nick woke he would find her gone, as savagely removed from his life as he had once been from hers.

But before leaving she returned to his bedroom once more. He still slept, and she moved silently to the unit that stood beside his bed, placing the two hundred pounds where he couldn't possibly miss seeing it when he woke up, quietly leaving the room and the house afterwards.

CHAPTER NINE

SHE was working later that morning when the insistent ringing began on her doorbell, taking her time in going to the door, not sure that she was up to this confrontation yet. She hadn't slept at all after she returned to her apartment last night, the time she had spent in Nick's bed shaking her more than she cared to think about, and meeting him again now, when her defences were down, wasn't something she exactly welcomed. But this final meeting had to be faced, and perhaps it was better sooner than later.

'What the hell do you mean by sneaking out of my bed and house in the middle of the night like that?' he didn't waste time on preliminaries, striding arrogantly into her lounge to glare across the room at her. 'And what's the meaning of this?' he threw the folded twenty pound notes down on the coffee table between them.

It was as if he had thrown down the gauntlet between them, reminding Danielle of the reason why she had carried out this elaborate plan of revenge. She stiffened her shoulders in resolve, ready to face any of the fury he might show her with an anger of her own.

'I didn't sneak out of the house,' she told him coolly. 'I simply left; we both know I was well enough.'

His eyes iced over. 'It wasn't a question of whether or not you're well enough, you know damn well that after last night we needed to talk.'

'Why?'

He drew in an angry breath. 'Because last night was the deepest, most satisfying lovemaking I've ever known. And it was *your* lovemaking.'

She looked at him coldly. 'Not too mechanical for you?' she taunted.

Puzzlement flickered in his eyes at the bitterness he detected in her voice. 'Look,' he began in a reasoning tone, 'I know you're angry with me, that we argued before we made love. But I *know* you felt the same completeness I did.'

She shrugged, knowing she couldn't deny it. 'Isn't that what sex is all about?'

'No!' He was breathing heavily in his anger. 'And it wasn't just sex.'

'Wasn't it? I thought we had acknowledged before we went to bed together that that was exactly what it was between us,' she drawled dismissively.

'Danielle——!' He sighed the frustration of his anger. 'Why did you leave the money? You were a guest in my house, I didn't expect you to pay for your bed and food.'

'Oh that money wasn't for my food,' she looked at him steadily, waiting for him to realise what it had been for.

'Then what——?' He seemed to become suddenly still as realisation hit him, swallowing hard. 'Are you saying you left the money for last night?' he asked softly.

'Isn't it enough?' her tone was deliberately provocative. 'I realise that the rate for a whole night is probably a little higher than that nowadays, and of course there's always inflation, but——'

'Danielle!' He shook her roughly. 'You're talking hysterically.'

'Am I?' she looked at him with contemptuous green eyes. 'I thought I was perfectly calm.'

'*Too* calm,' he grated. 'And you aren't making much sense either! I want to know what significance that money has to us.'

Want. *He* always wanted. Well right now *she* wanted him to leave her alone, the revenge she had wanted leaving her trembling and weak after waiting seven years to achieve it. 'Think about it, Nick,' she derided. 'Perhaps you'll remember.' She moved out of his grasp, able to breathe again.

'I want to know *now*.'

Her eyes flashed dangerously. 'And I don't feel like telling you,' she rasped. 'Just give it a little thought,' she taunted, 'I'm sure a clever man like you never forgets a thing. Now if you wouldn't mind,' she added pointedly, 'I was working when you arrived.'

'But I do mind,' Nick grated. 'I mind very much. I want to know what the hell is going on?'

'And I want you to leave,' she stated coldly.

'Danielle, whatever else is going on here—and I wish to God I knew what it was!—I love you.'

An emotion akin to pain ripped through her. His love, if she could believe he meant what he said, had come seven years too late. Once she would have welcomed such a declaration, would have been grateful for his support while she carried his child, but it was just too late. 'I'm sorry,' she said flatly, her expression emotionless.

'I want to marry you!'

She flinched. That too had come too late. 'I'm sorry about that too.'

He gave a choked groan at how calm she sounded. 'You really mean this, don't you?'

'Yes.'

'Last night meant nothing to you,' he realised dully. 'It was exactly what you said it was, you just wanted to go to bed with me.'

'Yes.' Her confirmation was only slightly slower in coming the second time.

His expression was harsh, his face pale. 'You don't even like me very much, do you?'

'Have you liked every woman you've ever been to bed with, desired?' she answered him with a question of her own.

'Of course I liked them——'

'Let's put it another way, do you *remember* them?' she cut in heatedly. 'Do you remember the women you've slept with?'

'I don't—I'm not on trial, Danielle,' he defended harshly.

'Then perhaps you ought to be,' she dismissed coldly. 'Yes, perhaps you ought to be. You walk into a woman's life like a conquering hero, and walk out again just as quickly when it suits you to.'

His eyes narrowed thoughtfully on her flushed face. 'Did I once hurt someone you know?' he asked softly.

'Someone I know?' she repeated with distaste. 'Yes, I suppose you could say that.'

'What was her name?'

'Ellie,' she revealed flatly.

He frowned. 'Ellie What?'

'Oh no, Nick,' she said sharply. 'I'm not going to do it all for you, Take your—your money,' even talking about it sickened her, 'and leave.'

'It isn't my money——'

'Oh, yes,' she nodded grimly. 'It is.'

'I don't understand.'

'Like I said, Nick,' she picked up the money and thrust it into his hand, 'think about it. I'm sure that somwhere among that calculator you have for a heart you'll remember.'

He crushed the money in his hand, staring at her. 'I do love you, Danielle,' he said gruffly.

Her gaze didn't flicker as she stared straight back at him.' And I don't love you.'

He heaved a ragged sigh. 'I can't leave with things like this between us.'

'I'm afraid you'll have to,' she dismissed without emotion. 'I don't want you here.'

A nerve jerked in his rigidly held jaw. 'Did you go out with me because of this Ellie woman?' he grated.

'You're very astute, Nick,' she mocked.

'And very stupid,' he ground out.

'Never that, Nick,' she said hardly. 'Never that.'

'Oh yes,' his eyes were narrowed. 'Stupid enough to fall in love with a woman who doesn't even like me.'

'Maybe that was my attraction for you,' she taunted. 'I've heard that willing women pall after a time.'

'You would never pall for me, willing or unwilling.'

Her mouth twisted. 'I'm sure you tell that to all your mistresses.'

He stiffened at the taunt. 'You haven't believed a word I've said, have you?'

'No,' she derided.

He strode angrily to the door. 'Don't think I've finished with you yet, because I haven't!'

Danielle wasn't in the least perturbed by his warning, knew that once he realised she was 'the little whore' he believed his niece had found him for the night that he would have nothing further to say to her.

She had intended all along to tell him exactly what he had done to her, had meant to tell him of his daughter he had had no interest in, but when it came down to it she hadn't wanted to tell him anything, knew that she would be hurt more by telling him about their baby than he ever would be. Her daughter had been precious to her, and she didn't want her memory sullied by anything Nick said about her. No, she had given him back his money, felt confident that he would eventually remember the young girl he had once paid to go to bed with him. It was enough.

She left the apartment as soon as Nick had gone, needing to be completely alone now that it was all over. Could he have really meant it when he told her he loved her and wanted to marry her? As far as she knew Nick had steered clear of any emotional entanglement since his divorce, had admitted himself that he never felt anything more for his mistresses than expediency.

But she had steadfastly refused to become his mistress, had made him wait before going to bed with him. Could it possibly be that by waiting he really had fallen in love with her? How ironic if he had!

The haggard-faced man waiting for her when she returned from her drive bore little resemblance to the arrogantly confident Nicholas Andracas she had become used to!

It was late when she returned home, almost eight o'clock, and from the look of Nick he had been waiting most of the eight hours she had been out. Could he possibly have remembered so soon? And if he had, what was he doing here?

Neither of them spoke as she unlocked her door, Nick following her inside to sink down gratefully

into a chair, looking greyer then ever. Danielle
woodenly poured him some brandy, watching as
he drank the whole glassful down in one swallow
without so much as flinching.

There was naked pain in his eyes when he finally
looked up at her. '*You're* Ellie,' he said raggedly.

She nodded, refilling his glass, pouring some for
herself this time, grateful for the warm fluid as she
sat down in a chair opposite him.

He looked at her with dazed eyes. 'I only ever
knew one Ellie that I could remember, a beautiful
young girl with long corn-coloured hair and
wistful green eyes.'

'Wistful?' she echoed sharply.

'They seemed that way to me,' he sighed. 'When
I first looked at you—seven years ago.'

'Then you do remember?' she rasped.

'Yes,' he confirmed roughly, drinking some
more of the brandy. 'I remember you very well.'

'Now,' she mocked harshly.

He sighed. 'I had no reason to connect the
sophisticated portrait painter Danielle Smith with
a young girl I once——'

'Paid to go to bed with you,' she finished hardly.

He flinched as if she had physically hit him.
'That's what the money was you left for me last
night?'

'Yes.'

'You kept it all this time?'

'I'd never been paid for making love with a man
before!'

He stood up jerkily, his hands thrust into the
pockets of his fitted trousers. 'What I did to you
that night was wrong, I know that, but at the time
I had no reason to believe——'

'I was anything more than a paid whore your

niece had acquired for you,' she finished hardly. 'What a charming family you are!'

He drew in a ragged breath. 'You have a right to feel bitter about that night, to hate me for it, I realise that.'

'Do you?' she scorned. 'I doubt it!'

'I wasn't thinking straight that night,' he rasped. 'I just wanted to hurt someone.'

'Me!'

'As it turned out, yes,' he sighed. 'Let me tell you about that night, Danielle——'

'I know all I need to know about it, thank you,' she refused tightly.

'I know there's no real excuse for what I did to you,' he said softly. 'But I didn't realise—I had no idea until after you had left of the real injury I had done you.'

She gave him a sharp look. 'What do you mean?'

The grey eyes were sad with regret as he looked at her. 'You were a virgin.'

Danielle turned away, paling slightly. 'How do you know that?'

'I was far from gentle with you. There was some evidence of that in the bed, and——'

'Oh,' she blushed her embarrassment of the physical evidence he had found of her virginity, having read about such things but never believed it had happened to her, the pain she had felt too brief to have done any real damage.

'I'm sorry, Danielle,' his expression showed his regret. 'I don't want to distress you any more than I need to about that night.'

'You won't,' she told him flatly.

'Danielle——'

'I'd rather not talk about it any more!' She

looked at him coldly. 'The debt has now been paid, I want to forget all about it.'

'But *I* can't,' Nick rasped. 'I may have been blinded by bitterness and anger when we met seven years ago, but I can see clearly now, and I know I love you. I want to marry you.'

'And it must be obvious by now that I have no interest in either one of those things!'

His gaze was compelling on her angrily flushed face. 'Danielle, I may have just wanted to vent my anger against my wife on the nearest available woman seven years ago, but what was your motive for going to bed with me?'

She couldn't meet the merciless probing of his eyes. 'You were Nicholas Andracas,' she shrugged with a nonchalance she was far from feeling—and they both knew it. 'I was overwhelmed by the fact that you had singled me out for your attention.'

'Like hell you were,' he bit out grimly. 'Tell me the real reason, Danielle. Please!'

'I—You were attractive——'

'The real reason, Danielle,' he repeated forcefully.

She shook her head in denial of the pressure he was exerting on her. 'If you're expecting a declaration of love out of me for what occurred that night you're going to be disappointed,' she derided bitterly. 'I didn't want or expect you to take me to bed that night.'

'But you were powerless to stop me, weren't you,' he persisted gently.

'You were far stronger than I was——'

'And you didn't even try to stop me,' he reminded softly.

'The mood you were in it would have been futile!'

'Yes,' he sighed at the truth of that. 'My wife had decided to file for divorce, and I was furious about the conditions she made. I had to agree to be the guilty party when I wasn't, and she wanted a huge cash settlement. Neither condition exactly hurt me, but I despised Beverley's method of getting her own way.'

'I'm really not interested in the failure of your marriage,' Danielle told him distantly. 'Or the reason for it.'

'But don't you see, it's all connected to that night I hurt you so much?' he demanded impatiently. 'I had received the divorce papers from Beverley only that morning.'

'Carly had already told me that you had some unsettling family news,' she dismissed.

'I'm sure she didn't tell you exactly what that news was, or that Beverley had made it clear I had better agree or else.'

'Or else what?' Danielle asked in a puzzled voice; she couldn't imagine Nick letting himself be blackmailed into doing something he didn't want to do!

'My wife—Beverley, had access to certain information that she knew I didn't want made public,' he revealed roughly. 'I agreed to her terms, but not without a certain amount of frustrated anger on my part. I was ranting and raging to my niece Carly about how mercenary women were, and how I would rather know up front that I was paying for the privilege of bedding her. Carly thought it was very funny, told me that if I wanted a whore perhaps I ought to get myself one.' He looked at Danielle with pained eyes. 'You left the party with me so willingly, raised no objection when we went to my apartment, that I thought you were Carly's idea of a joke.'

'And I said nothing to make you believe any different,' she recalled dully, remembering the strange and not always comprehensible conversation they had had that night after he had made love to her.

'I should have known,' he grated. 'Your look of innocence was too real to be the faking of a professional, your bewilderment afterwards too genuine. I came to my senses a little while I was in the shower, decided I should talk to you, find out who you really were. But of course you had gone by the time I returned to the bedroom——'

'You told me to go!'

'Yes,' he sighed. 'It was then that I realised the full extent of what I'd done to you. I realised then that far from being hired by my niece you must in fact have been one of her guests. I telephoned her with the intention of finding out more about you, but before I could say anything she started teasing me about going off with one of her school-friends——'

'*Finishing*-school,' Danielle cut in determinedly. 'I was nineteen!'

'Nevertheless, I was left with the feeling that I had seduced a child, that I had brutally taken your innocence, searching you out then would have got us nowhere. I had made a mistake with you, but I didn't love you, had nothing I could offer you to erase that memory from your mind, could give you only more embarrassment about the error I had made. I decided it would be better if we just forgot the incident. But you haven't forgotten it, have you, Danielle?'

'No.'

'Neither had I, not completely. Oh I buried the

memory at the back of my mind, but it was always there.' He shook his head. 'It's a little late to apologise now, but I'm going to anyway. I never meant to hurt you, Danielle.'

She remained aloof from the warm pleading in his voice. 'As you said, it's a little late for apologies.'

'Danielle, you said the debt had now been paid,' his voice softened encouragingly. 'Couldn't we start again, with none of this between us?'

'No!'

'But I love you,' he groaned huskily. 'I love you so much. I'd do everything in my power to make up for the past. Won't you even give me a chance?'

Her mouth was tight. 'I said that debt had been paid, Nick,' she rasped coldly. 'But there's another, much worse one, that I can never forgive.'

He frowned, his eyes narrowed questioningly. 'Are you talking about the way I lost my temper last night and forced you to make love with me?'

'We both know it wasn't force,' she derided.

'Then what?' his voice rose as he held back the frustration of his anger. 'Danielle, you have to tell me what else I've done to you!'

'I didn't intend telling you anything,' she scorned. 'But you came here expecting a few words of apology to make everything right between us. But it never will. You see, you say you had nothing to offer me after that night,' her voice cracked emotionally. 'But a little moral support from you then would have wiped out all the misunderstanding of the past. Put quite simply, Nick, you let me down when I most needed you, and I couldn't trust you now not to do the same thing again. I wouldn't even have wanted you to marry me then, just not let me go through all that alone,' she added contemptuously.

'You mean people found out about that night?' he frowned his puzzlement.

'Of course they found out,' she scorned.

'Did Carly tell——'

'*No one* told anyone anything, Nick,' Danielle rasped bitterly. 'No one needed to. A pregnancy is a difficult thing to hide.' She looked at him unflinchingly, the whole truth out now.

Nick seemed to go very pale, almost grey, his expression haggard. 'I didn't make you pregnant, Danielle——'

'Then who do you think did?' she scoffed harshly.

He swallowed hard, pain flickering in the depths of his eyes. 'Are you saying I was the father of your child?' he asked disbelievingly.

'I'm stating it as a fact,' she glared at him.

He closed his eyes for a moment, shaking his head. 'Danielle, I couldn't have made you pregant——'

'Oh no?' she taunted hardly. 'Just wait here for a moment.' She ran into her bedroom, quickly finding the three things she wanted, taking them back into the lounge to hand them to Nick. 'I realise none of these things are "conclusive evidence",' she mocked. 'But they're all I have— besides the fact that I know I've never slept with any other man but you.'

Nick looked at her searchingly for several minutes before turning his attention to the things she had handed him. He looked first at the medical card that had accompanied her each time she visited the doctor, the weeks and date of her pregnancy clearly stated. His hands shook slightly as he moved on to the next paper she had given him, the birth certificate of her daughter, with his name clearly shown under father.

He looked up, swallowing convulsively. 'You named her Nicole,' he said dazedly.

Danielle hardened her heart against how shaken he was. 'Choosing *my* daughter's name was my prerogative,' she told him coldly.

'But you called her Nicole,' he repeated determinedly, as if the knowledge were precious to him.

Her eyes flashed deeply green. 'Don't read any deep significance into that,' she snapped dismissively. 'I just happened to like the name.'

His breathing became ragged as he looked down at the last object she had given him, the miniature she had painted of their daughter. 'She——' he ran a hand over his eyes. 'She looks so small,' he finally choked.

'She was,' Danielle told him woodenly. 'Too small.'

His eyes seemed overbright as he looked up at her. 'Danielle, I had no idea—I couldn't have guessed——'

'You didn't even bother to find out!' she accused heatedly.

'For a very good reason.' He drew in a controlling breath. 'Danielle, my marriage had been far from happy for some time before the divorce, and although my wife wanted to leave me I refused to let her, didn't believe in divorce. My wife used the one weapon she had to force me to release her. Danielle, she used the fact that I was incapable of giving her a child.'

She became suddenly still, searching the pale

harshness of his face, seeing only the intensity of pain in his eyes, the way he held on tightly to the miniature he still held. 'Why would you believe such a lie?' she prompted softly, suddenly filled with uncertainty.

'She did lie, didn't she,' he stated fiercely.

'Yes,' she answered him simply. 'Nicole was definitely your daughter.'

'A daughter my ex-wife convinced me I could never have!' he rasped. 'No wonder you hate me. God, I have to—I have to be alone for a while. Please—please excuse me.' He pushed the miniature into her hand with the medical card and birth certificate, leaving before she could attempt to stop him.

In that moment Danielle felt a compassion for him she had thought she could never feel for such a man. For seven years Nick had been under the misconception that he was incapable of being a father because his ex-wife had lied to him to achieve her freedom. The shock of now finding out about Nicole must be tearing him apart.

Nicole. She had lied when she told Nick she just 'happened' to like the name. She had deliberately chosen it because it was the nearest female version to his own name, to the name of the man she had loved despite his desertion of her.

And she loved him still!

CHAPTER TEN

THAT knowledge didn't come to her in a blinding flash, she knew with startling clarity that it had always been there, pushed to the furthest recesses of her mind so that it didn't cause her any more pain. But she had loved Nick seven years ago, and she loved him now, knew that was the reason she wanted him to be angry when he made love to her last night; his gentleness would have been the breaking of her.

How her heart suffered for him now, for the pain and disillusionment he must be going through after seven years of believing himself infertile to know that her daughter, the child that had so angered him when he found out of her existence, was his own daughter. How could any woman, for whatever reason, be so cruel as to tell a man like Nick he was incapable of being a father.

Nick was the sort of man who would have wanted a big family, sons and daughters to carry on the Andracas name. And he would have been a good father to them too. The fact that Beverley Andracas had got away with her lie all these years was a cruelty that must be tearing Nick apart.

But the pain of believing himself infertile was now over for him, and he would start to think of a future for himself once that knowledge hit him. The question she had to answer was where, and if, she fitted into those plans.

There could be no doubt that she loved him, deeply, that she had never stopped loving him. But he had hurt her once, more than she cared to think about. Admittedly, she could now understand his behaviour a little better, could even feel pity for what he must have suffered, but she didn't know if she could ever give him her love so trustingly a second time. In her confusion she wanted to see the only people who could maybe help and advise her.

Her father was drinking whisky when she was shown into the lounge, her mother shooting him concerned glances, which wasn't surprising when he hardly drank.

'I don't quite know where to start,' Danielle began tentatively.

'With Andracas, I should imagine,' her father growled.

She frowned. 'As a matter of fact, yes.'

'I knew it,' he snapped. 'Ellie, I don't——'

'Thomas, you said you wouldn't interfere,' her mother gently reminded him.

'I know,' he scowled. 'But I can't sit by and watch her ruin her life over a man like him.'

'I think you should both know that Nick has asked me to marry him,' she told them quietly.

'Marry him . . .!' her father repeated dazedly.

She nodded. 'Yes.'

'Good God—marriage!' her father rasped. 'I thought the man was a confirmed bachelor. You told him no, of course.'

'Thomas!' her mother frowned at him, obviously able to read more in Danielle's expression than he, anger blinding him to anything but his own disapproval. 'Let Ellie speak.'

He still looked angry, but at least he was quiet now, glaring belligerently at the whisky in his glass.

Danielle moistened her lips, nervous now that she had both their attention. 'First of all,' her voice sounded very harsh in the silence. 'I didn't meet Nick for the first time a few months ago, I knew him before that.'

'But——' a warning look from her mother once again silenced her father. 'Go on,' he muttered.

'Seven years ago,' she added pointedly, waiting for their reaction to that.

Her father seemed speechless suddenly, her mother finally the one to answer. 'Ellie, is he——' She began again, very pale herself now. 'Is he——'

'Nicole's father?' she finished gently, hoping to lessen the shock. 'Yes, he is.'

Her father swallowed what was left of his whisky. 'He was married seven years ago,' he grated.

'In the process of being divorced—because of his infertility,' she added softly.

'Tell us everything, Ellie,' her mother gently prompted.

As she did so she felt her own anger towards Beverley Andracas grow, finding the trust for Nick that hadn't quite been there this morning.

She had been as much in the wrong in the past; knew now, and had known then, that Nick would never have denied the existence of his own child, even without the fact that it would have proved his ex-wife a liar. Her own pride, in the fact that he couldn't love *her*, had been what had denied them being together then.

And it was only pride that prevented them being together now, using the grudge of the past to deny them the happiness they could have together. Pride was only a fleeting emotion, being with Nick was to be alive, fully, vibrantly alive.

'And I want you both to know,' she concluded with a new resolve. 'That if Nick still wants me, I'm going to marry him.'

'You love him,' her father stated flatly.

'I always have,' she nodded. 'And this time he loves me too.'

Her father took her in his arms to hold her tight. 'If he's what you want then he's what we want too.'

'Thank you, Daddy,' there were tears in her eyes as she hugged him.

'And I expect to be able to give the bride away,' he added sternly. 'The man's arrogant enough to just take you!'

She laughed happily. 'And I may just let him.' She sobered suddenly. 'But I have to find him first. He was very upset when he left me.'

'He's strong enough to bounce back,' her father assured her.

She hoped so, she sincerely hoped so. There could be no doubting that Nick was a strong man, but even he couldn't be expected to take the news of his daughter's birth, and death, calmly.

Barnham had no idea of his employer's whereabouts when she phoned the house, and although he could have been lying by instruction— she doubted Nick wanted company just now!—she didn't think he was. Which only left the apartment.

She received no answer to her knock, but when she tried the door she found it was open, going quietly inside. There was no evidence of Nick's presence in the lounge, and yet she knew he was there, could smell the cigars he always smoked, finally tracking him down to the small study she found off the lounge, seated behind the desk, his head buried in his hands.

'Nick.'

He looked up at the sound of her voice, his face haggard, his eyes bloodshot. 'Danielle,' his voice sounded strained.

She moistened her lips with the tip of her tongue. 'I've brought you a present.'

He seemed to stiffen, sitting straighter in his chair. 'Oh yes?' he was very wary.

She reached into the pocket of her denims, taking out the small tissue-wrapped object. 'I want you to have this,' she put it down in front of him on the desk, stepping back.

His hands shook slightly as he slowly unwrapped the object, staring at the miniature of Nicole as it lay flat in the palm of his hand. As Danielle watched and waited for his reaction she saw the tears start to fall down the harshness of his grooved cheeks.

'Oh, Nick!' she choked, running to put her arms around him, feeling him shudder against her as he buried his face against her breasts, sobs wracking his body. 'Nick, it's all right, darling,' she soothed, hating to see this strong man bowed by his own grief, but knowing that it was a necessary part of the healing process. 'It's all right, Nick,' she repeated firmly as she felt him regaining control.

His arms tightened about her. 'Why are you here?' he asked gruffly.

'To give you your daughter. And me too, if you still want me,' she added uncertainly.

He looked up at that, the ravages of emotion still evident in the pale harshness of his face. 'You're the one thing I can't live without!' he groaned his need.

Her hands framed his face as she bent to kiss

him. 'I feel the same way about you,' she told him between kisses. 'I love you, Nick. I love you!'

'Are you sure?' humility didn't sit well on his broad shoulders. 'I've hurt you very badly.'

'You were hurt more yourself.'

'Damn Beverley to hell.' He stood up agitatedly, moving away from her. 'I telephoned the specialist in New York that we were both dealing with,' he spoke woodenly. 'He told me that both Beverley and my tests were positive, that there was no reason either of us shouldn't physically have a child.' His hands clenched at his sides. 'He also told me that Beverley had been on the pill for most of our married life,' he ground out. 'That she had a psychological aversion to having children. She lied and deceived me for over five years, got me to agree to be the guilty party in our divorce because she knew I couldn't take the humiliation of being publicly branded infertile. She played on my self-conceit—and I fell for it.'

'And now?' Danielle prompted softly.

'Now I could wring her neck for what she did! I was in London when the results of the tests were available, I believed Beverley when she told me she had seen the specialist and he said it was my fault we could never have a child. And at the same time Nicole was already forming inside you.' He looked at her with tortured eyes. 'I would have wanted my daughter, Danielle.'

'And what do you want now?' she persisted.

His eyes darkened almost to black. 'You. I just want you. Will you marry me?'

Relief flooded through her. 'I thought you would never ask me again!' She ran into his waiting arms. 'Of course I'll marry you,' she told him eagerly.

'Tomorrow?' he groaned, his arms closing about her convulsively.

She touched the hardness of his cheek with gentle fingertips. 'I don't think things can be arranged that quickly in this country,' she said regretfully. 'And my father insists on giving me away,' she added lightly.

Nick frowned. 'You've told him about us?'

'I've told both my parents about you.'

'God, they must hate my guts too,' he sighed.

'I told them everything, Nick,' she said gently. 'And they understood.'

'Then you must have very sympathetic parents,' his expression was grim.

She shook her head. 'No one could blame you for what happened in the past.'

'Not even you?' his gaze avidly searched her face.

'Not even me,' her arms tightened about him. 'You were right about my motives, Nick, I did love you seven years ago, I would never have gone to bed with you if I hadn't.'

'I know that. Now,' he sighed his regret that he hadn't realised it then. 'I was so wrapped up in my own bitterness I couldn't see anything else.'

'It doesn't matter now, can't you see that?' she prompted gently. 'We love each other, and we have all of the future to show each other that, starting now,' she added enticingly.

'Not here——'

'Exactly here,' she looked up at him unflinchingly.

'But what happened here last time!' He looked as if the thought pained him.

'That's the reason it has to be here,' she smiled. 'We have a few ghosts to exorcise.

'You're sure?' he still looked uncertain.

'Very,' she took his hand and led him in the direction of the bedroom. 'This is a change,' she teased. 'It's usually you trying to drag me to bed!'

His mouth quirked into the ghost of a smile. 'I just want everything to be perfect between us this time.'

'Everything *is* perfect between us,' she assured him. 'And it can only get better. Trust in me, Nick,' she encouraged as she began to unbutton his shirt.

His eyes were almost black with emotion. 'Can you trust me, that's the problem? I let you down once when you most needed me, how can you be sure I won't do it again?'

She stripped the shirt off his shoulders, letting it fall to the ground, feeling the way his body leapt with response in spite of himself. 'I know you well enough now to know you would have been at my side if you had known about the baby. Neither one of us can continue to brood about the past, about what might have been, we have to go forward, Nick, or not at all.'

His arms moved about her as he crushed her against his bare chest. 'I couldn't live without you, Danielle. For God's sake don't leave me!'

'I never will,' she promised.

'My marriage to Beverley was a matter of expediency, a business merger that never worked because we just didn't love each other. But I'll love you for the rest of my life,' he told her fiercely.

She knew that, knew that once his love was given Nick would never take it back. And he had given it to her.

'You were wonderful, darling,' Nick lifted the hair

at the back of her nape to kiss her, his dinner jacket discarded on a chair, his shirt partly unbuttoned.

Danielle turned into his arms. 'A dinner party for ten of your business acquaintances is child's play compared to being your wife,' she dismissed teasingly.

He looked down at her with warm grey eyes. 'Has the last six months been so difficult for you?'

It had been the most wonderful six months of her life. Nick treated her as if she were the most important thing in his life, and he was certainly the most important in hers. Only one thing persisted in marring her complete happiness, and after all this time it was something she tried not to think about too often.

'Not bad,' she gently mocked him, wrapping her arms about his neck, feeling his instantaneous response to her nearness even as she felt her own senses stir. 'Not too bad at all really,' she teased.

'Not bad!' he groaningly derided the description, burying his face in the throat. 'You make me feel guilty enough to take up the reins of my business again, and now I have to invite those people tonight because I'm so rarely at the office this is the only way they can get to see me!' he said wryly.

'I don't make you stay at home,' she feigned innocence.

'You don't exactly kick me out of bed either,' he said dryly.

Neither of them had done much work the last six months, the slightest excuse giving them reason to stay at home together, and as Nick said, it was usually in bed. 'I'm not so stupid to deny myself that pleasure,' she gave him a smile that spoke of remembered satisfaction, none of their heated passion for each other fading the last six months of marriage, in fact it seemed to have deepened.

'Talking of pleasure. . . .' He looked pointedly in the direction of the bed, the two of them having shared the master bedroom in the Andracas house since their return from a month's honeymoon on Nick's yacht.

Danielle never argued with him when he suggested they make love, and after showering together in the adjoining bathroom they became immersed in the pleasure of pleasing each other, passion quickly rising as urgency possessed them.

She felt the usual sense of disappointment as Nick momentarily left her to open the drawer in his bedside cabinet. As he turned back to her she wasn't quick enough to hide the wistful expression in her eyes.

He became suddenly still beside her. 'What is it?' he said sharply. 'Darling, what's wrong?' he frowned.

She forced herself to smile naturally, entwining her arms about his neck. 'What could possibly be wrong?' she said throatily.

Uncertainty flickered in the depths of his eyes. 'For a moment you looked—sad.'

'You're imagining things——'

'No,' he spoke with his own haughtiness. 'Danielle, tell me what's wrong.'

She sighed, recognising his determination to have an answer. 'I prefer to make love to you without the interruption of—contraception,' she admitted huskily.

His face became shadowed. 'You know the doctor advised you not to go on the pill.'

'Yes,' she sighed again.

'Danielle?' he prompted gently.

She evaded his gaze. 'It's nothing.'

'If it bothers you then it's something,' he persisted.

She chewed on her bottom lip for several seconds before turning to look up at him. 'I would prefer it if we didn't have to use contraception at all,' she met his gaze unwaveringly.

Nick seemed to pale. 'What are you saying?' he said gruffly.

'Darling, I know we never discussed it before we were married,' she smoothed the rigidity of his cheek. 'And perhaps it's just that you don't want us to have children just yet, but I don't *know* how you feel about it!' she finally spoke of the one thing that had darkened the horizon for the last six months, Nick always careful not to take any risks of their having a child.

'You want children?' he looked at her searchingly.

'Don't you?'

'I'm more interested in your answer,' he evaded.

She bit her bottom lip to stop it trembling. 'I thought you would want children,' her voice quivered emotionally. 'I thought——'

'Darling, I do,' he folded her tightly in his arms. 'But after Nicole I didn't want to put you through that heartache again just for the sake of my male pride.'

'Nicole dying was an accident, Nick,' she comforted him in a voice that was beginning to lighten with hope. 'She was just born too early. There's no reason to suppose it would happen with another baby.'

'I couldn't be sure you would want another baby.'

'I want one, I want several, maybe half a dozen,' she added with a catch in her voice.

'That's ambitious,' some of the tension began to ease from Nick's face.

'You can do it, darling,' she lightly teased, the shadow fading as she sensed his own eagerness for a child.

'*We* can do it,' he corrected throatily. 'Maybe we'll have the first one by Christmas if we start now.'

'That's only ten months away!'

'I'm ambitious too,' he murmured before his mouth captured hers, the two of them soaring up to the plateau of ecstasy they always enjoyed together.

THE
Leo Man
Rebecca Stratton

THE Winds
of Winter
Sandra Field

Love Beyond
Reason
Karen van der Zee

Man
of Power
Mary Wibberley

4
FREE
Harlequin Romances

TAKE THESE 4 Harlequin Romances FREE

Delight in **Mary Wibberley**'s warm romance, MAN OF POWER, the story of a girl whose life changes from drudgery to glamour overnight....Let THE WINDS OF WINTER by **Sandra Field** take you on a journey of love to Canada's beautiful Maritimes....Thrill to a cruise in the tropics—and a devastating love affair in the aftermath of a shipwreck— in **Rebecca Stratton**'s THE LEO MAN.... Travel to the wilds of Kenya in a quest for love with the determined heroine in **Karen van der Zee**'s LOVE BEYOND REASON.

Harlequin Romances . . . 6 exciting novels published each month! Each month you will get to know interesting, appealing, true-to-life people .... You'll be swept to distant lands you've dreamed of visiting .... Intrigue, adventure, romance, and the destiny of many lives will thrill you through each Harlequin Romance novel.

Get all the latest books before they're sold out!

As a Harlequin subscriber you actually receive your personal copies of the latest Romances immediately after they come off the press, so you're sure of getting all 6 each month.

Cancel your subscription whenever you wish!

You don't have to buy any minimum number of books. Whenever you decide to stop your subscription just let us know and we'll cancel all further shipments.

Enter a uniquely exciting new world with

Harlequin American Romance ™·

Harlequin American Romances are the first romances to explore today's love relationships. These compelling novels reach into the hearts and minds of women across America... probing the most intimate moments of romance, love and desire.

You'll follow romantic heroines and irresistible men as they boldly face confusing choices. Career first, love later? Love without marriage? Long-distance relationships? All the experiences that make love real are captured in the tender, loving pages of **Harlequin American Romances.**

What makes American women so different when it comes to love? Find out with **Harlequin American Romance!**

Send for your introductory FREE book now!

Get this book FREE!

Harlequin American Romance

Twice in a Lifetime
REBECCA FLANDERS

Mail to:

Harlequin Reader Service

In the U.S.	In Canada
2504 West Southern Ave.	P.O. Box 2800, Postal Station A
Tempe, AZ 85282	5170 Yonge St., Willowdale, Ont. M2N 5T5

YES! I want to be one of the first to discover

Harlequin American Romance. Send me FREE and without obligation *Twice in a Lifetime*. If you do not hear from me after I have examined my FREE book, please send me the 4 new **Harlequin American Romances** each month as soon as they come off the presses. I understand that I will be billed only $2.25 for each book (total $9.00). There are no shipping or handling charges. There is no minimum number of books that I have to purchase. In fact, I may cancel this arrangement at any time. *Twice in a Lifetime* is mine to keep as a FREE gift, even if I do not buy any additional books.   354 BPA NAZJ

Name   (please print)

Address   Apt. no.

City   State/Prov.   Zip/Postal Code

Signature (If under 18, parent or guardian must sign.)

Exclusive Harlequin home subscriber benefits!

- SPECIAL LOW PRICES for home subscribers only
- CONVENIENCE of home delivery
- NO CHARGE for postage and handling
- FREE *Harlequin Romance Digest*®
- FREE BONUS books
- NEW TITLES 2 months ahead of retail
- MEMBER of the largest romance fiction book club in the world